TALL AIR

12/19
BOB— Thanks
for your
support... hope
you Enjoy!

Tall Air – Here is what they are saying:

"High Speed, Low Drag! What an AMAZING ride!"
- LCDR Jamie "Tilly" Tilden, Washington

"I could never adequately explain the reality of my days in middle and high school to my daughter. Your description hit the nail on the head."
- Penny McCready, Harbor Springs

"I loved it—laughed, smiled, and even got a little teary. Hot fire, hot guys, some pain, and a lot of sympathies."
- Curl Candler, Traverse City

"Yes, the '60s were something else, and Stone and Finn sure extracted their fair share—the good and bad— as we all did."
- Robert Johannes, Colorado

"You had me totally in the cockpit and I don't know anything about flying. The smell, feel, and emotion are there—loving it on the edge of my seat. More please!"
- Tom Patterson, Lake Orion

"Your passion is so real—your enthusiasm is contagious."
- Jack Haughton, Bloomfield Hills

TALL AI

Artwork by · **John R. Doughty, Jr.**

R

Solid Friends, Fractured Times... Growing up in the Sixties

D. Stuart White

Knighthawk Publications

Knighthawk *Publications*
Bloomfield Hills, MI

Tall Air may be purchased for business, educational, or sales promotion use. For information please email to wa2dsw@gmail.com.

Contact Information:
Knighthawk *Publications*
Orders – wa2whiteassociates.com/
Website - dstuartwhite.com/
Wa2dsw@gmail.com

Library of Congress Cataloging-in-Publication Data
White, D Stuart, 1944
Tall Air
FICTION / Thrillers / Military
FICTION / Thrillers / Historical
FICTION/Action & Adventure
Library of Congress Control Number: 2019915438

ISBN: 978-1-64438-049-9

First Edition 2019

Dedication

This book is dedicated with love to my wife
Ann Carlton White,
"My Soul Whisperer;"
To my son Andy and Lauren and their brood,
Maddy and Evan; To my
Sister, Linda, and brother Bob;
To my father,
LT David E. White,
"More than a driver of a B-29"
And my mother, Betty Ann.

And finally: To the fallen in worldwide conflicts and
to those still fighting their wars.

Acknowledgments

The author owes much to the following people in the creation of this novel. Their contributions, edits, useful comments, suggestions were many, not only for Tall Air but for his personal growth. Thank you: Ann White, David Aretha, Pat Kilkenny, LCDR Jamie "Tilly" Tilden, Nabin Karna and Stephan Beale, Clifford Gillespie, LT David E. White "Daddy Addy" Addison, Andrew David White, LTJG Daniel Heming, MSLCA Members, LTCOL Robert McVey, Captain "One Ton" McCready, and the 1963-1969 MSU Lacrosse Teams.

Contents

Introduction

The War Never Stops—It Just Drips On
You'll Never Walk Alone" – Mormon Tabernacle
Choir/From Carousel

He's so quiet. I'm not used to his silence—I miss the endless stream of banter. But I get it. Who wants to go through this? I wait with him while he gets the poison pushed into his veins. We play cards and talk but mostly he just sleeps. It gives me a lot of time to think, to remember. There is a lot to remember. So much of it makes me laugh—other memories, not so much.

Chemo—I try not to let him know I'm worried. I guess we are all afraid we will have to face this. But my pal—no way! Always active, healthy, and full of spit.

Time has sure done a number on him—in my mind I see that square jaw, cleft in his chin, dark penetrating eyes and a smile the ladies could not resist. Now his face is gaunt and creased. His eyes have lost their spark and he is thin, way too thin. He wearily peers over at me and I see something in his face I have never seen before—he is afraid—trying his best to mask his fear. He was the the best of us and now—a shadow of his former self. This is just not fair! Why hasn't anyone figured this disease out? This makes me so angry! He does not deserve this!

As Mathe (Māthe) dozes off I pondered the cause of his cancer. They think this might be his exposure to Agent Orange in Vietnam, but no one is sure—or they just aren't saying—and I wonder how many other guys are going through this. At least I can be here for him. We've had each other's backs for as long as I can remember. Where else would I be?

He lost his dad in WWII. What little he remembers of him he has never discussed. His mom's scrapbooks and his feelings are stashed away—he keeps them tightly wrapped. I have had my dark times too, but not like his. He doesn't think that I see his sadness. His fight for health only seems to amplify the pain he's endured.

He has always taken on his burdens and confronted his tragedies directly and has reveled in many of life's pleasures. We have explored and shared much together, and I watched his career in aviation blossom from our first civilian flying missteps to NAVAIR flight competence.

After leaving the Navy he chooses to lead a so-called " normal life" to find a real job in the corporate world. Even so, he eventually found Tall Air again by transitioning into corporate jets as a contract pilot — or until a few months ago.

After a long career, filled with challenge, as a Naval Aviator, I chose another path—retirement. Mathe and I still find time to fly in the reserves and competitively test our selves together.

I have never held the fact that he spent time at U of M against him. We Spartans have always been less misguided in life's social, intellectual, and political orientation than our friends on the other side of the tracks. At least we think so. Go Green! And—if it helps him—Go Blue!

I guess there are a lot of reasons why God put us together. We are similar to the neural connection that binds us, yet very dissimilar at the same time. For all his self-confidence, I was a bit lacking. He was fearless in everything. I was always hesitant about jumping in and seemed to see the down side in most of our adventures—and of course, he saved my ass way more than once. For all his dark good looks I guess I'm the other side of the coin—blond-haired, blue- eyed, a bit gawky but well-intended. But if you flipped the coin you might just see both of us as one.

We each have had our own time in the barrel—I wouldn't be here at all if it wasn't for him. I would have missed my whole life.

Although our friendship started long before, it was our military experience that was the real cement. For some, the dream gets smashed. For a few, that dream of flight never ends. It was our common bond, for the effort—the wanting it—to test ourselves, to struggle, and to succeed in the pursuit of the end.

I turn my head and look at him lying there in the chemo chair—as I watch the drip, drip, drip into the black and blue vein on the top of his hand. "Hey, buddy, our 'Gotta Get There' list is growing. I have some great ideas for our next one."

"Yeah, sounds good to me, pal."

One: The Two-Headed Coin

Burdens Carried
"Father and Son" – Yusuf/Cat Stevens

1970 Vietnam

The wind racing by his canopy brought Finn back from his temporary dream state, on his letdown to the boat off the coast of North Vietnam. He couldn't hold onto consciousness and wondered if he was bleeding out. Had Mathe's calls brought him back?

Captain Matthew (Māthe) "Rock" Stone watched his buddy L.T. Jonathan "Finn" Finley's descent, as he rode his wing from a distance, and helplessly watched the rapidly decaying control of Finn's aircraft. "Hold it together, pal. We're almost home," called Mathe, as he watched the fuel stream drain out of Finn's aircraft—way too close to his jet's exhaust.

Finn tried to keep his head up. Holding onto hope, he took a glance at the gauges to reconfirm his problems. He felt the energy getting sucked out of his machine and himself and pressed his mic button. Holding onto hope, his fingers found the appropriate buttons and knobs inside the cockpit to fight his emergencies—but he knew he was rapidly succumbing.

"Mathe, not sure I can stretch this glide to the boat," he said, trying to sound confident.

Finn slowly rolled the "scooter" towards the shore, thinking that his chances for survival were better over land. He was well into North Vietnam, and he would find a way out into the safety of the South. Blood in the water on an ejection was the last thing he wanted after hearing stories of aggressive shark populations off the shoreline. Finn's mind raced.

He continued to stare out of the cockpit into the empty sky ahead and felt as if he was not there. Time seemed to compress as he held the stick a little tighter and alternated between accepting his fate and fighting for his life.

Vice-like fear crept in and out of his thoughts for his chances of survival as his G-suit torso seemed to be tightening by itself. He was slowly releasing the pressure of speed, time, altitude, distance, fuel, and system calculations—common flying concerns just seemed to fall away. The inner battle to give in to his emotions, to scream and leave the work for someone else, to just steer the machine was getting stronger.

Deep in North Vietnam airspace, in a heavily damaged fighter, lieutenant Johnathan"Finn" Finley thought to himself: *Don't take the easy way out—work to survive your wounds. You have support, the ship is waiting for you, and Taco and Mathe are on your wing— you will make it.* Then there was the other voice—but then…

The Engine Fire Warning Light suddenly blinked intermittently and then glared full-on from Finn's A-4 Skyhawk instrument panel—and told it all.

"My God! Fire! God no! Not today, not now—please!" Finn yelled.

He thought he heard the crackle of hot metal from the rear of the airplane and felt the heat rising. A small wisp of smoke rose from the cockpit floor, and the jet jumped. He was suddenly watching the dirt and everything else, on the cockpit floor rise to eye level and suddenly drop. It only took a second.

Mathe followed Finn's jet down, on his wing, looking over at him in shock and horror, and the frustration of not being able to help his pal. It was eating him alive. Suddenly, Finn's father's words—spoken to both boys long ago—popped into this head:

"Boys, don't let yourselves ever become a two-headed coin—you will never win! You probably have never seen one, but they were common in my era, and they can be much trouble if a lot is riding on the flip. You guys are very much alike—more than you are dissimilar in many ways. A two-headed coin can be a powerful tool in the wrong hands, so be careful with your abilities and the direction you take in life. Sometimes the wrong-decision paths are easily taken."

Finn was frozen, caught between covering every inch of ground to the safety of the sea and the carrier Raleigh (CVA-23) in his rapidly decaying machine—and the reality he didn't want to admit: his firecracker of an airplane could explode at any moment. Coming to his trained senses, he slammed the PCL (power control lever—the throttle) off, pushed the fuel shutoff lever to emergency off, and pulled the emergency generator handle to extend.

Holding on for dear life, he yelled to his jet, "I need fuel now but fire, no, no, no."

Finn fought for control, held the stick tighter, squeezed her harder—trying to get the attention she was not giving him—to control her, to fight her if he had to. Even so, she yawed into a rapidly decaying roll and spin. The fog bank below was about to swallow both of them, as he continued to strain and yell for control of the machine.

Finn's survival vice—holding onto life but fighting the opportunity to leave—was reaching critical mass. Eject before it is too late, he told himself. Mathe and Taco's voices were screaming at him to punch out—but held on for a little more distance—ever closer to his aircraft carrier, or was it shore? Confused and in and out of consciousness—he wasn't sure anymore.

Losing consciousness for a moment the jet suddenly departed flight again and began to tumble with fire enveloping the cockpit. Finn's jet was now flying backward—a true ass ender.

"Please, God, get the nose to come around, out of the flame so I can leave," Finn cried.

The hot rod slowly begins to turn it's nose toward the fog bank—down.

He's beyond worrying about the pilot who makes no mistakes—the close-to-perfect pilot, in his mind—the most consistent OK three-wire grabber in the squadron.

"I need to live," he cried, and suddenly, "God, I have no control!"

"I can't save the plane and not sure about me," he mumbled.

Calm took over Finn—nothing mattered much to him now. Not the pain in his groin and cheek, the heat and fire; not the green color security of his jet's cockpit, the locker room/cockpit smell of oil, jet fuel, sweat, nor the dry, rubbery on-demand O2 he breathed. His concern for the wind whistling through the holes in his airplane—underneath and right beside him—didn't seem so important now.

There was Captain Matthew (Māthe) Stone, fellow "Talon" and buddy, frantically, giving him hand signals while flying next to him and Taco, in trail, yelling for him to eject.

Mathe joined in, "Finn get out! Get out of the airplane now!"

Two: California Boy – The Hardening and Softening

"Here Comes the Sun" – Beatles

1954

I turned 12 on the road trip here, and somehow Mom found a bakery and cake in some little town on our travels east to Michigan. It was three weeks before school started and the summer was already getting old. Too much time riding my bike searching for fun and new friends.

We had just moved to the Midwest, and it was a far cry from the fun and sun of Pasadena, California. Mom said Michigan, was the land of cold, snow, and cars. There was no sign of cold or snow yet. My dad's new job was with Chevrolet, so there we were. Guess they call it the suburbs—safe schools and a safe place to raise kids and all that stuff, she said. A little too quiet for me too! And not California!

Yeah, I had a younger sister, but after convincing her she could fly off the garage roof (resulting in her broken collarbone) I was not supposed to play with her. That was OK. I didn't want to anyway.

The trip from Pasadena to Michigan had been fun—after getting over the idea of leaving home.

"Why do we have to leave without Flaps? He is part of our family. We really didn't leave Flaps, did we, Mom?" I pleaded.

Mom told us that our Cocker Spaniel Flaps was with friends, that there were plenty of space for him to roam and that we would visit him. Eventually, the hurt would go away, but we sat devastated at the time, not understanding that our best friend wasn't in the back seat with us as we pulled out of our Pasadena home. So, off we went—uncharted territory ahead.

Dad was still trying to exorcise his WWII flying demons and both Mom and Dad sought out friends to socialize with on a nightly basis. The pain of the war hung over many as each veteran and family sought a new life without the horrors of war. Mom seemed to have turned into a heavy cocktail-drinking bridge card-game, party fanatic who left my sister and me to run freely and to grow on our own terms in Pasadena. I guess the pain of the war years created a need to escape. Looking back, it seemed understandable that giving birth to me and the next week hearing that my dad was lost in China after bailing out of a B-29 would drive anyone to take life a little easier when they could—and for two newly married 24-year-olds the time was now for both of them. I hoped that would change in our new home but held little hope. Even so, it was a merry bunch that piled into the Nash seeking a new life in Michigan.

The animated neon restaurant signs and cowboy bars merged into a never-ending flow of root beer and hamburgers with more fries than we could eat. Log cabin motels in the middle of the desert hills—a new place to sleep each night with arcades, fairs, and rodeos around every corner—fun stuff to see and do on our two-lane Route 66 path to Detroit.

As I positioned my hand to zoom upward and then dive in the hot summer air outside the window of our car, I peered over Dad's shoulder at the road ahead and daydreamed.

"What is our new house like? Are there any kids?" I kept asking. Mom and Dad did their best to dodge the question.

"You'll see, just wait," they kept repeating.

"Last Chance" this, "Last Chance" that seemed to appear on every sign we passed—and I started to get nervous. *What was coming that I didn't know about?*

As we motored through the black desert night a glow behind the next foothill caught my attention. My mind crept to visions of flying saucer landings and little green men. We finally passed over the hill's crest, and I spied my first real desert city. It spread before me in a spectacular lighted array. Street lights were twinkling and stretching for miles with a distinct edge that turned black abruptly against the night. We passed the city and traveled out of the light and eventually turned into our Last Chance Motel, a dingy oasis on the outskirts of Flagstaff.

I felt the temperature change as we traveled "out east" deep into the Midwest. The land turned green with fields of corn and wheat. What a huge amazing country. Finally, we arrived "home"—all different and new to me—a quaint, well-to-do suburb just northwest of Detroit.

It was so much slower here. The house next door was empty, and on the other side was an old couple. They were nice, I guess. They made us cookies. But as far as I could tell, no kids my age anywhere—I didn't get it. There was a baseball diamond behind the church, but no one was ever on it—ever. The school playground, only three blocks away, was empty most of the time or just moms and little kids on the swings. There was one kid down the street—Timmy something or another, but he just wanted to read books. Not what I was looking for! Really needing a friend prompted me ask one more time: "Mom, can we get a dog?"

Our new neighborhood was different from Pasadena. Really huge old trees lined my new street. The sun was never scorching, but the air felt wet—and almost no wind—what a strange place. Where could I get a taco? Beans and rice would do. Boy, did I miss the salty, pungent kelp beach smell of Southern California. My senses were getting hammered with all this green vegetation—trees, bushes, and green grass—not like the entirely burned Pasadena lawns I knew—and sadly, no mountains.

The memories are so vivid just like they were yesterday. I was in my room again, by myself, lining up my toy soldiers for another battle when I heard an airbrake gasp. A big truck pulled up next door.

I was instantly glued to the window, as the men started unloading stuff on the lawn of the empty house: bed frames, chairs, boxes—you know, the usual. Then I spied a bike— a boy's bike! A blue Chevrolet Bel Air station wagon pulled up and parked behind the truck and a lady got out. Then out of the back, a kid my age! Scruffy looking, long hair—jet black hair, as dark as the grape jam Mom spread on my toast in the morning, dirty T-shirt, jeans, and a pair of well-worn Jack Parcel sneakers.

Mathew Stone was short—I was not, but that was OK.

I ran down the stairs, flying out the door, and in his face before you could count to ten. We took a look at each other and just knew—the beginning of a long friendship. He actually held out his hand and told me to call him Mathe (Māthe).

I smiled. "Hi, I'm Finn."

I didn't dare to tell him Jonathan was my real first name—Jonathan Finley. I did not want to be called Jonathan!

As we shared notes, I looked over at his stuff stacked on the sidewalk and saw a strange-looking stick with a net attached—some kind of racket I guessed.

"Hey, Mathe, what is that thing?" I asked, pointing to the stick with a net on the end—or whatever?"

"You really don't know what that is? It's a lacrosse stick—I will teach you how to play. Come on, grab something and help me get this stuff inside. You need to show me around."

He later told me he was from Pennsylvania, where he and his mom had lived on a small farm after his dad died in the war. I said I just got here too—from California. We were the same age and would be going into the same grade this fall. I gave him a rundown on our new town and told him there wasn't much to do.

He said, "We'll fix that."

In those three weeks before school started Mathe and I must have put a thousand miles on our bikes.

We put a jar of peanut butter, bread, and a couple of apples in a bag and WERE GONE! My mom kept asking where we went all day.

I always answered, "Nowhere in particular."

But the answer was everywhere. We found kids, lots of them, back at the ball field, the corner drugstore, all over the place. They said they were back from camp or from "Up North," wherever that was. And they actually wore shoes—new for a California boy! Eventually, I saw those green trees' leaves turn yellow and orange and drop to the ground, and then SNOW—a whole new season to explore.

Mathe liked everything I liked and more. Together we were a force to be reckoned with for our parents, the school, and the local police.

We never really worried about getting caught by the police or sent to the principal's office, for the real threat to our misadventures came from our parents—and they were huge. Dad's strong suggestion, and forceful power to enforce put some teeth in "don't get caught." It made simple sense. We developed almost a sixth sense at pulling the plug on our adventures when we sensed getting caught was real.

We pursued each of our whims with a vengeance—wherever they took us. Slingshot fights with occasionally broken windows were shared as we rode off on our badass bikes. They sounded like Harley motorcycles, from the clothesline pins holding playing cards that flickered against the spokes of our wheels.

While being chased down the street by the town bullies one day, Mathe got caught. I stopped half a block away and fought my fears of the beating I would take if I rejoined Mathe to help. I realized that it was easy to be brave from a distance, or a chicken in my case. So, I got some gumption and closed in on the bullies. I knew he would have helped me.

I jumped right in front of Mathe thinking I could bully the bullies and got immediately pasted. It was the first time I had ever been hit, and they got the better of us—but we survived.

As we finally disengaged, bloodied and all, Mathe gestured, "Well, that sure went well"—as he picked my ass off the street.

He was always hanging it out, pressing the limits. He was probably also wondering how long he would have to continue to jump in and save my ass. Slinking back home, we swore never to let this happen to us again—ever.

We didn't realize it, but the beat down seemed to give both of us a new, hardened approach to our schoolmates. Mathe now wore his rugged hostility all over his sleeve.

Whatever we did together, Mathe always seemed to do it harder. At times, I was sure he wouldn't survive some of our frays—but he perpetually did.

He was like a brother to me. We did everything together: explorations into the local forest and lake, taunting the local girls in front of the soda fountain, playing hockey all day and returning home with slowly thawing, painfully frozen feet. Fighting off older bullies from school was usually followed by running harder from them than turning to face a fight. In little league football games—more like wrestling, pushing, and shoving matches with boys from neighboring towns—we had an edge.

Even though Mathe had a friendly side, he was also secret, often too quiet—a tough nut to crack. It would take me years to understand what was driving his demons.

Our play was ongoing and included inserting lilacs into fences to camouflage our fort behind the garage while waiting to shoot up the imagined Nazi troops charging our position. Many times we hid in corner attics talking about forbidden secrets or playing doctor with willing neighbor girls. Running races between us to see who could beat not only the school bus home but each other was ongoing. But he was always at my house, raiding the fridge and teasing my sister. Later in high school we usually picked short term girl friends for what was stocked in their parent's refrigerators. Even so, Mom could never figure out where all the food went.

Eventually, hormones became a force. We tried to cope with our newfound urgings and to control their awakening impulses. Encouraged by our mothers to participate in ballroom dancing classes, we laughed at our awkwardness in approaching our female classmates. Girls at that time were nothing more than a curiosity, but we came to realize their importance in very individual ways. Their more balanced behaviors and approach to their days, against our entirely expansive approach to life, gave both of us enough curiosity to provide them with a chance—and in time gave us much more for our souls than we had bargained.

Mathe and I had been playing hockey all day at the local lake—you know, nonstop pickup games and challenging the speed racers on their course next to our shoveled hockey rink—and getting drubbed. Of course, their blades were longer than ours. At least that was our excuse for the continuous second place we took.

When Dad, David Finley, was a teenager, he lived in the big house on the west side of our town's only lake. He called it "The House that Chevrolet Built." Dad grew up knowing marble floors, multiple servants, and a hidden staircase from the living room to Grandpa's bedroom.

You see, Grandpa worked for Chevy in the early '30s and was key in the strategy development to divide GM into multiple divisions—under the GM umbrella. He was so good at motivating dealer groups that Chevrolet negotiated an agreement whereby he received a dollar for every vehicle sold. Dad lived there until the corporation gave Grandpa a Nash dealership in Pasedena.

This was the lake that took Dad's dog, Skipper, one sad afternoon when he was growing up. He told me of watching Skipper walk out on the thin spring ice, break through, and then struggle while yelping for help for what seemed like an eternity. Skipper was a hundred yards out, and the pain of watching him try to survive and then pass under the ice hurt for years.

Our deep sea (actually, lake) adventures included building tire inner tube rafts and tying them together from vines pulled from the overhanging lake trees. We fantasised that we were deep sea explorers as we paddled our homemade craft near shore to search for adventure. Oh, the 50s…

Three: Limits and Mastery

A Mother's Pain
"I'm Eighteen" – Alice Cooper

Middle school was like being marooned on some planet. No one knew who they were, what they were doing, or why they were doing it. There were some in my classes who looked like they were 10 and others who you thought should be high school seniors. We spent our days trying to be "cool," whatever that was, and not succeeding very often. Studying was real work as far as I was concerned. I had to hit the books to get OK grades. Mathe, of course, never seemed to crack a book and got good grades. Sometimes he drove me nuts.

But, middle school provided more avenues for laughter and young fun. The mandatory first period naked boys' swim class in the schools cold pool gave us the opportunity to point and gawk at each of our classmate's boyhood.

The girl thing hit full bore at age 13. It wasn't all Jerry Lee Lewis's fault, but he and several other bands sure had a hand in it—that heightened state of tension and expectation that ensued, while not being sure of what to do about it if the chance arose. You know what I mean.

Gym class provided the first real direct stimulation, with new feelings brought forth in the floor-to-ceiling rope climb. Many could not finish the climb, not for lack of strength but a sudden overpowering pleasurable weakness in our groins. I was a three-knotter and could not overcome the feelings, while some made it to eight knots high before succumbing. My first "rising" in class was very disconcerting. How do I walk out into the hallway with this?

Mathe, walking out of the class from across the hall, looked at the embarrassed discomfort on my face and the position of my books and said, "Got one, eh?"

"Yeah, Mathe, how about you?" And we both broke down in laughter.

Recess in middle school included smear games. You know it as dodgeball, but it was a more vicious version in our day. Two sides on a tennis court with each team trying to knock out the other players by hitting them with a ball—of course, as hard as you could heave it.

It was all-out war for both of us. Why dissect frogs in biology class when we were going to do the same to our classmates on the smear court? We discussed tactics in the morning on the way to school, the movements of other players, whom to destroy first, the dislike for one and not another, ball-throwing techniques and girls we might impress if we knocked out the right players.

The game was notorious for leaving many with bloody noses, sprained ankles, torn shirts, and pants. Mathe and I were vicious in our attacks. A ball to the kisser for those who could not duck fast enough and for those we felt needed a refresher in manners or a simple beat down brought us joy. We ruled with the smear ball.

We were warriors—even though we knew inside that we would never be better or less than our schoolmates who showed up every day.

We were all trying to find ourselves—searching for our paths in life to make our half-formed dreams come true. And I felt each was working and growing through the smear experience to achieve it. We were learning our limits and figuring out what we could and could not control.

As I limped back into the classroom after our usual smear lunch break, I caught the teacher shaking her head while looking at my torn-out jean knees, shoulder rips, and bloodied nose. I shrunk, for phony protection, and she smelled fear.

She looked at me like I was mad, out of my mind, but was not sure how to handle the situation. As the intensity of our noontime battles increased, it was apparent that the games would have to stop. Maybe showing horror movies/action movies in the gym during lunch would be the solution, our teachers thought—and that is what they did.

High school was always there with its "Don't do this and don't do that" monotony. However, we found ways to sprinkle it with the laughs we generated from the constant pranks played on fellow students and teachers. School was a place to be tolerated from the real adventures we found away from its restrictions. Our goals seemed to be different from others, and we vigorously pursued them while biding our time in public education. We learned more about ourselves and girls outside than in the false rigors of our teacher's lesson plans and the school's structure and process.

After dragging my tired butt home after another full day in the cold— skating and trying to deal with the pain of thawing toes, my dad commented, "Oh, by the way, a girl called you. I didn't catch her number. She said you knew her." I looked at him in disbelief, and he said, "And I think her name is Jane."

I knew who she was and her reputation, which was all I needed. Suddenly I was no longer tired, nor did my toes ache for some reason, as a new expectation rose instead. Totally forgetting what I looked and smelled like, I redressed in my hockey uniform thinking it would impress her—for what I wasn't sure. It was just a new heat that said *let's find out* that drove me. I furiously peddled my bike through newly fallen snowdrifts and underneath the street light shadows to reach her house. My lust drove me faster into the night as the words *Would she? Will she?* kept repeating in my mind.

After skidding on her icy driveway, I threw my bike down, jumped to the doorstep, and breathlessly knocked on her door. She opened the door and gave me a big smile. Jane was cute but still lacked the raging beauty of some of her classmates. Blond hair, a pretty look, and an accepting smile told me all I needed to know as I gave her a hug and barged into her house. I could tell she was lonely as she grabbed my arm and pulled me into the hallway. I quickly asked her if her parents were home and she looked at me and responded with a willing smile. I did not pursue the answer for it really did not matter.

Well, we talked and laughed, and for some reason I missed every cue she threw my way. Girls—I hadn't a clue about them. I was counting on my primal urges to give me direction—to cover my inexperience. I started to take off my equipment—one hedonistic, lusting shin, shoulder, and hip pad at a time. It was hot with all this equipment on, I quickly convinced myself. Suddenly, the headlights of her parents' car illuminated the driveway after swinging across the front yard and then centered on the garage door at the side of the house.

"Oh my—geez," I mumbled in panic.

And with a flurry, I became a fully dressed hockey player again—just making a friendly visit to a teenage girl whose only need was a conversation in her lonely, insecure world. Someone to talk to, to tell her she was OK and maybe even loved.

After several years I looked back and realized it was so simple, yet at the time I wouldn't have understood what I had just surmised. Jane's reputation was not based on any real experience disclosed. Only perceptions of those cruel enough to dislike her for no good reason—only the high school gossip that freely flows among teenagers that can kill reputations and create massive pain for the recipients of trumped-up perceptions. While pedalling home, I wondered if Mathe was having similar experiences.

I knew Mathe had problems at home. Mathe told me about his mom and the disruption she was causing in his life and what he thought were the demons that were driving her.

The abuse he took at home vented itself in his drive to push himself—to seek escape in athletics and physical activity, to not face the pain he was experiencing. He confided in me at times. He said he was ready to burst and leave but he could not abandon his mom. He said he couldn't take any more of her hungover breakfasts before school, black eyes from her falling down when she was drunk, the insanity of her requests that many times did not make any sense, and most of all her verbal and physical abuse that she would inflict for no reason.

He frequently hunted for liquor bottles around the house—just like an Easter egg hunt except a lot more dangerous. One afternoon after school he was watching TV in a back room to escape the drunken howling of his mother. She found her way to the den and, while booze enraged, she started beating down the door, which he had locked to keep her out. It did not stop until the door burst off the hinges. After that, he shut down, ate his anger, and talked very little about her again.

I think he wished he could reach inside her soul to drive her pain away. He just could not help her and he was terribly sad about it.

'You know, you only get one mom, Mathe."

"Yeah, I know. I do love her but I sure don't like her."

Was it because they lost the farm—and they had to move? He looked so much like his dad—did this reminder drive her pain? I guess some broken hearts just never heal.

Four: Water Tower Boys

Death Zone Explorers
"Born to Be Wild" – Steppenwolf

1959-1963

Slowly, we imagined ourselves into a different life. I know Mathe needed another. He was strong, good looking, and driven from within to succeed on his terms. I was OK following his lead but I seemed to be a bit unaggressive at times and needed coaxing to jump into the fray. But like a rope, I didn't unravel or become worn at the edges.

Most of all, Mathe and I challenged each other in new ways as we grew through our middle and high school years. Even though he was shorter, I looked up to him and he did the same to me.

Each new adventure got bolder and more demanding. We lived to better each other, and the dangers in each experience only increased with time. Each foray left us completely alive—entirely in it.

"Got the nads for this, Finn? You're not scared, are you? "Mathe often yelled.

Caught between my fear of failing and Mathe's perception of the challenge always left me thinking: Am I just ordinary? Am I not strong enough to take this on?

The higher the angle of the roof, the more significant the challenge to reach the top. We climbed the highest peaks of the buildings in town to see who would make it to the top—who would chicken out first?

Many times it was apparent that the climb was not worth the risk, and we would stare at each other and acknowledge the seriousness of the situation and begin our descent—not discussing what we hadn't accomplished. We both shared the excitement and sought out the tallest in each of the surrounding neighborhoods.

One night, while on the roof of one of the more reasonably pitched buildings in town, we saw the next challenge at the same moment. Why we hadn't thought of it before this, I will never know. We had been riding our bikes by it for ages. A very tall, huge, scary-looking water tower—we had to climb it!

"Let's go for it," Mathe said.

My smile was my answer.

We reconnoitered the water tower for the best time to climb so our illegal adventure would not be detected and our butts not land in jail and made a pact to meet the coming Friday night. While the town was at the local high school football game, the tower would be ours. That Friday came fast. I didn't say much on the way there—cold feet for sure, but hey, I promised, right? So with a bit of old rope, worn-out sneakers, and dark clothing, I watched Mathe put his foot on the ladder and climb like some lizard. Now it was my turn.

About 40 feet off the ground, I suddenly could not move my arms to the next rung. Sweating profusely, frozen to the step, and stuck entirely to the ladder, I stared at the safety of the ground. Mathe looked down and could see my confusion and he alternately shamed and encouraged me.

"Come on, Finn, you can make it. Don't look down. Look at me! Come on, you big baby, move your legs. Climb, you pussy! You will never live this down if you stop!" Mathe yelled.

The term "young and dumb" was given a new meaning that night.

I was holding on to each slippery rung of the ladder more tightly than ever as the soles of my shoes threatened to slide out from under me on each upward step. My toes seemed to be trying to grip the ladder through my shoes as my fear took hold. With one handhold and step at a time, I moved ever so slowly upward.

* * *

Vietnam – 1970

What Finn didn't know but suspected was that he was losing blood from his wounds.

The wind racing by his canopy brought Finn back from his temporary dream state on his letdown to reach the carrier off the coast. He couldn't seem to hold onto consciousness in the descent. Reaching the coast or any "feet wet" egress point always brought more safety than having to face the enemy on land after an emergency ejection. "I'll have a chance if I can reach the coast—please God, let me get to the water," Finn screamed.

Mathe watched Finn's descent and the rapidly decaying control of his aircraft and wondered if he was going to make it. His jet was a mess and so was Finn.

"Hold it together, buddy, we're almost home," called Mathe, as he watched the fuel stream drain Finn's aircraft—way too close to his jet's exhaust.

Finn tried to hold his head up, and a glance of the gauges reconfirmed his problems. He felt the energy getting sucked out of his jet and himself and pressed his mic button. His fingers holding onto hope found the appropriate buttons and knobs inside the cockpit to fight his emergencies—but he knew he was rapidly succumbing.

* * *

I finally found my way to the top edge of the tower and proceeded a slow-walk to a higher peak. Mathe punched my arm with a contagious smile as we searched our town from our new 360-degree perch.

"You're such an idiot, Finn," he said as he punched me again.

While sitting quietly on top of the tower, admiring the view and measuring our success, I suddenly felt the peak's top ball cap move. If it *moved* it could be *removed*, right? So one tower at a time we began collecting them as trophies. We began roping these sixty-pound steel caps off the top of each tower we climbed. Getting them down and back home was more difficult than climbing the towers, but we did it. Our tower top cap trophies began to appear under bushes in each of our backyards and key places around town—and somehow we never got caught. Our climbing conquests increased along with our trophies.

We were fascinated by these water tower mountains and fantasized that we were part of the fraternity of climbers that summited the tallest mountains on Earth.

We were the death-zone explorers without any panic-stricken bad memories, and we kept going up.

However, one water tower scared the living shit out of us. Maybe this was our fifth tower climb in a neighboring city. I don't remember. The tower was not different than the ones we had previously climbed except for one detail. The tower metal ladder was wet from the night's rain before. What I do remember, very clearly, was slipping from the ladder rung 30 feet in the air. I held on with just one arm as I reached out to Mathe and yelled for help. He was below me but not by much.

Mathe saw my fear as I dangled and then suddenly lost my concentration and slipped off the rung. The fall didn't break my neck, but my arm was broken. After seeing his friend fall, Mathe rushed off for help.

Later in the hospital, with my arm bound tight to my body and the side of my face bandaged to cover more stitches, I knew it could have been worse. Laying in the hospital I caught the turn of Math's head as he looked at me and we laughed—I was still alive and kicking it. My laughter told him I would be ready to try it again—very soon.

From this point on my fears were fewer and in most cases gone as we continued to challenge each other in new ways. Individually, we were strong, but together we were amazing. I guess it was the coin thing dad kept warning us about. We won at everything. We weren't bullies. We just excelled at whatever path we took. Water tower climbs would receed for us as we found other ways to grab Tall Air.

Five: Insecure Moments

Walking a Razor Blade into Adulthood
"Going Up the Country" – Canned Heat

In many ways, our parents, without knowing it, gave us the strength to challenge authority in the '60s. As kids, we learned to value freedom above all else and pursued it with a vengeance as adulthood hung over our heads. Of course, walking the razor between responsibility and just screwing off was part of growing up. We knew what was expected of us. We just didn't always like it.

In the context of the times, we did a lot of stupid things—it was the '60s. As college decisions approached, we felt the need to visit select college campuses. Mathe was hoping (DU) the University of Denver would accept him and worked out a time to visit campus—a western road trip. We could combine it with some skiing—in fact, much skiing—at key ski resorts in several states.

Mathe had set up an interview at DU, and some of his past high school buddies who attended CU set up the ski trip. So I offered my wreck of a car, with the outstanding sound system, to drive us out. The interview made the trip legit as far as our parents were concerned. Mathe provided all the marijuana we could smoke. I didn't ask where he got it but knew of his contacts at school. You could always find some if you asked the right people.

He needed the scholarship they were offering and had to seal the deal as soon as possible with a face-to-face admissions meeting. College was not in the bag for Mathe. A scholarship was the only way he was going to get there—and he did. In spite of our hijinks, he excelled in almost every academic endeavor he attempted.

The trip provided an opportunity for high schoolers to get away, and we were eager to try this new experience—while smoking dope. With my old Chevy's sensational stereo playing full blast, time disappeared as we rolled along the interstate—west out of Chicago to Denver.

"Finn, this is too much fun. Let's go all the way into Los Angeles after I finish the interview. You game?" He smiled.

"You bet, Mathe—a real road trip tacked on to a college admission run and a ski trip," I slurred.

Before I lost it entirely in a weed fog, I thought of all the jobs I'd worked to cover the cost of this trip with the result being a newly trashed savings account. Riding a tractor and changing fairway sprinklers all night at the local country club, with a bucket of Cokes and a hidden bottle of vodka, made things interesting. My dad got us the job. I would rendezvous with James, a fellow high school student, by the 10th green around 10 p.m. and it got hilarious. We listened to the radio broadcasts of professional fights while hiding from the greenskeeper in the bushes along the side of the course—sipping vodka Cokes. The summer before, while working the line as a riveter at the local truck plant, was hard. Trying to maintain the line speed while completing my assigned station tasks was a challenge. The lunch breaks at the local bar and the pressure to get out and back to the line with side bets of who could drink the most bottles of beer in the allotted 45-minute break time was probably the more significant test.

We kept the window rolled up as we laughed our way to Denver. Eventually, we needed gas and more snacks. I cracked the windows open as we got out at the next gas stop. Even in our haze, we both looked back at the car with smoke rising out of the partially open windows and broke up.

As I watched Mathe stumble around the gas pump trying to fill the vehicle, the sweet smell of weed kept pouring out of the car. I smiled. Could it get any better than this?

Mathe's college buddies at CU were itching to start our ski road trip and were waiting for us to arrive. The trip would take us through Colorado, Idaho, and Wyoming to every major ski area. However, all Mathe and I had to do was get to Denver for the meetup, and we would be on our way.

Mathe and I, and some guys nicknamed Stinky, Forbush, Slope, and Magnus—four college students, a Malamute puppy, one pop-up camper trailer, and a pickup truck—pulled into the Vail City dump that first night. We claimed our parking space in highly sought-after accommodations. I thought my adventures with Mathe were wild and hairy but our fellow college adventurers rivaled and surpassed any ribald undertaking Mathe and I had experienced and we hung on their every word. Each mostly came from the East Coast to attend college in Colorado. *City boys gone mad in the clear mountain air*, I thought, but boy could they ski.

A cheap night camping was great and after the round of bar visits, with no success for additional companionship joining us, we found our way back to the dump. Someone pulled out a .22 rifle that they kept in the truck and started plinking away at the multitude of foraging rats that shared our campsite. At about 4 a.m. we all were awakened by the howling of our puppy and witnessed the side of the camper ablaze. Someone had left the Bunsen burner on to dry out some wet socks hanging over the flame. They eventually just dropped into the fire, and the canvas side of the camper quickly disappeared in flame.

Later that early morning we were hit by a snowstorm that completely covered the inside of the trailer. The drift was also right up to the lip line of one guy sleeping in the open pickup truck bed. His body inside his sleeping bag was completely covered with snow. All we could see was his pie hole sticking out from under the snowdrift with him snoring away—oblivious to the drifted snow and cold.

After each day's skiing, bar hopping, and camping, we reached the opinion that we were hopeless. And so "Hopeless Team Six" was born. No hope of comfort or success and completely irreformable.

My California roots didn't keep me from the ski slopes. I loved it—moving fast over a clean, cold surface, alternating between moguls for the quiet launch into blue crystal air. And I pushed it—always. I guess I was different from most. When trapped on a ski chairlift I decided to jump instead of the preferred move to wait for the repair. My chairlift buddy, a middle-aged man, lawyer type, stared down at me as I swung from one arm, skis polls and all dangling from the seat.

"What are you doing? Are you nuts?" he said.

"What is there to be afraid of," I yelled as I dropped from our 25-foot-high seat into a snowdrift. I smiled up at his look of disbelief, dusted myself off, and tooled on down the hill.

Launching off ski hill moguls and trying to stick the highest landings in surrounding trees was always an interesting challenge. It always ended with me grabbing for my life at each passing limb as I fell or ricocheted off the trunk or limbs into a snowdrift.

Oh yes, Mathe got the scholarship but turned in another direction, as U of M wanted him more. He eventually transferred to MSU to join James and me in more hopeless adventures.

Six: Flight Dreams

Seeking Tall Air
"Eve of Destruction" – Barry McGuire

I grew up with my parents' den walls covered with framed photos of Dad's WWII exploits. Throughout high school, they held a particular fascination. The images of B-29 and B-17 aircrews, AAF airplanes, battle scenes in the air, and crews posing in front of their bombers, both serious and smiling, captivated me. The most striking photo was a B-29 going down in a flare of flames and debris from a direct hit—a broken shooting star heading to the earth with its crew.

I was particularly fascinated with the aircrew photos—their smiles, comradery, heroism, and the challenges I surmised each faced to survive high-altitude flight—standing together beside their ships. They would become my perfect experience. My perception of their strength of character, courage, plus the pure freedom that flight provided became my goal.

I hoped these traits would inhabit my bones in time. I wanted to experience flight, and my dreams grew with each passing year as I pored through the albums my mom had so meticulously put together—their life together during their war years as newlyweds. Watching the TV series "Victory at Sea" only reinforced and glorified the romantic

31

notion that I would someday become a military aviator. I was hooked, and I would make this dream happen, and Mathe was right there with me.

Mathe and I continually searched for ways to go higher. We were going to make this happen.

Inspired by all these pictures, we pooled our lawn mowing money and bought a WWII parachute. We cut it up so it would look like the parasail/glider pictured in Look magazine. We hooked up a rope to the parachute harness and ran it to the rear bumper of my car. Mathe said he'd drive if I wanted to "fly."

"Can you handle this, Finn, or do I do the honors of the first flight?" Mathe shouted.

I smiled.

"OK, Mathe, here's a two-headed coin. Let's flip. We will both win if this works," I said and smiled back.

We then took turns running behind a car waiting for the parachute to develop lift—for the launch that never happened. The chute would extend lift for a moment; whipsaw us laterally back and forth in the air before throwing us to the pavement and dragging us until someone could signal the driver to stop. After several attempts that left us exhausted dragging behind the car, we continued the re-cuts of the chute for more lift—that never came.

Spectators lined the shopping center lot, and we heard much applause and laughs as we picked ourselves up each time from the bloodied pavement in our attempts to fly. Even so, we were undaunted by our failure—our chance would come.

High school girls Maddy, Gretch, and Rusty soon joined our group. We named them our "Motown Tall Air Queens" and wondered if they were interested in our adventures or just wanted to see us splat when we failed. Little did I realize how attached we would become to their company. For me, one would become a lifetime partner. For Mathe, well, I'll let him tell you that story.

Mathe had a thing for Rusty—a little red-haired firecracker that looked like his mom. Even so, he was so shy with girls. He never seemed to be able to relax around them. He had a lot of them interested in him, though. You know that silent rebel attraction thing. Girls seemed to love that shit.

Mathe and I found another Tall Air freedom searcher. I knew James "Gus" Jester from our summer golf course escapades, and I didn't hesitate when he asked me to take a ride in his new Porsche 911. As we drove down Woodward Avenue (the famous road to Downtown known for the "Dream Cruise") with one hand on the steering wheel and the other on a Coors, I marveled at how everything was perfect on this evening cruise. His family had money, and Jim truly fit the image of a spoiled, carefree 17-year-old trust fund type.

In a fit of bravado, to show me how cool he was, he suddenly reached into the glove compartment and pulled out a Colt single-action shooter and pointed it to the roof of his brand new car.

"Whoa, Jim, hold on. Is that thing loaded?" I stuttered.

Jim didn't miss a beat as he gave me his goofy grin, and before I could cover my ears, he blew a slug right through the roof of his new Porsche. The wind whistling by the open side window quickly cleared the gunpowder blowback as I tried to get smaller in my seat, nervously juggling my beer. Jim smiled and glove compartment holstered his piece.

"Jim, WTF are you doing? Are you nuts?" I stuttered in self-preservation. "Wait till it starts raining—you will regret that move," was all I could think to say. Our heads continued to swivel as we looked for cops. We laughed until we couldn't smile anymore—moving through stoplights toward Detroit and our Big Boy restaurant destination.

I seriously reconsidered my apparent envy of my friend. Maybe James's ability to not give a shit about anything was the attraction. Oh well, he sure was entertaining and just maybe I needed that in my life.

So, sure enough, it was a few years later when Jim and I were rolling through our college years, and the interior of his Porsche was finally showing rot from the moisture entering the vehicle through the repatched bullet hole. The bullet hole was his badge of honor, and many stories swirled about its cause over the years.

James, Mathe, and I made several static line parachute jumps in high school. With forged parent permission slips we secured our entry into the sky. We would not be denied. After a short one-and-a-half-hour ground training session at a local skydiving club, we got suited up. Finding courage in the C-172, without a side door, caused me to pause. The lack of a door just felt all wrong and startled me into the realization of what I was about to do.

At 2,500 feet I heard my instructor yell, "OK, Finn, get out of the airplane and stand on the wheel."

What was I thinking? I wasn't.

Holding onto the strut with one foot on the wheel and the other dangling in midair, I looked down to the ground 2,200 feet below.

What if I jumped and one of the pins in my backpack parachute got stuck, and I ended up dangling or banging against the fuselage of the airplane? Didn't want to think about that. Did I have the sense to pull the ripcord on my own? I looked back at Mathe and James, their smiles masking their fear, huddled in the rear of the plane—waiting to see if I would wimp out.

While standing on the wheel waiting for the signal to jump, I took another look down and had the same feeling I had on the water tower—absolute fear. Mathe could not help me this time. I was on my own.

"Jump!" My instructor caught my hesitation and yelled again, "Go now!"

I heard the words and hesitated—but not for long. Hadn't I always wanted to do this? I closed my eyes, let go, and fell into the slipstream. While trying to spread-eagle into a good stable fall, I went fetal and closed my eyes even tighter. The sudden pull of the risers let me know that I could open them—for I was momentarily safe.

I could not stop smiling as I looked for Mathe a couple of hundred feet above and behind me and gave him a Kiai (Japanese martial arts shout uttered when performing an attacking move) of pleasure. I failed to properly guide the parachute to the designated landing area and ended up in the middle of the narrow highway. Laughing, I picked myself up and gathered in the chute in my arms. A truck was bearing down on my position—honking at me to get out of the way as I scampered over to the side of the road. It was one hell of an adrenaline rush for me and pure joy. Mathe, James, and I met back up at the field and Mathe burst out laughing.

"You turkey, Finn—right in the middle of the road? Are you kidding me? If the jump didn't kill you, you could count on the truck." Mathe's bravado, his cover for the fear he felt—that cocky look in his eyes—had now been replaced with a new wild-eyed reality: that you could get killed doing this sort of thing. Two more jumps for all of us led to the realization that this activity was nuts. Besides, we have the Fourth of July right around the corner—always a blast.

As far back as I can remember the Fourth of July took on a very different dimension for our family. It was always a gathering of Dad's war buddies and stray pilots, who just couldn't kill the excitement gained from blowing things up. There were, of course, the usual sounds of firecrackers, M-80s, poppers, bottle rockets, and sky reports. Even so, they were drowned out by the occasional blasts of various .45 pistol shots, carbine clip unloads, the pop of trench guns, and captured German Mauser staccatos ripping the tree line and field beyond our house. Mathe and I reveled in these celebrations each year. We would walk the area the next day in search of spent shells and any creatures that had not been fast enough to get out of the way. We often talked about the day when someone would show up with a live grenade.

The war hadn't ended for Dad's WWII soldier friends, at least the blowing up part. This activity on the Fourth of July seemed to give each a release and the ability to come to grips with where each had been and the horror they had seen—an adrenalin pump that each seemed to miss. It was all good fun for them next to the backyard barbecue with liberal doses of Manhattans and beer to go around.

The local police knew of Dad's Fourth of July activities, but also knew that those blowing off steam were responsible and respected members of this small Michigan community. Together they had seen more war action than most of their fellow police officers, so Dad and friends got a pass. The police understood the need to release the war in any way possible, and they also knew these were fortunate men. They had survived and returned home.

Seven: Memories Stashed But Not Forgotten

WWII Reflections – David Finley
"Father and Son" – Yusuf/Cat Stevens

"Hey, Dad, can I be a pilot when I grow up?"

Over the years I had asked this question and he'd always found a way to dodge the answer or give no answer at all. It seemed to be his secret—pride or pain. I was never sure how he felt. Maybe he had suffered too much in the war and wanted to spare me the pain of what he thought I might go through if I chose to be a military pilot. The subject was always dropped. I was a stranger to his thoughts and his warfighter past.

Dad was fun-loving, a party jokester who loved skiing, dancing with mom, and the big band sound of his era. In high school, he was often called a real "hepcat." I often felt that under this persona hid a vulnerability that he kept to himself. To my sister and me he was a funny guy but had a hair-trigger temper that you did not want to cross.

He was somewhat aloof and uncommunicative with my sister and me. Even though he pretty much ran the show he deferred most household decisions — at least those visible to me to Mom. I always sensed that he knew I would seek out trouble in time—it was just part of growing up. So he was flexible and did not punish us often for our indiscretions. There was certain strength about him that I recognized and did not want to cross. The small number of rules I lived by were not to be broken for fear of physical punishment—even though I took them right to brink many times.

Both of our dads had been in the war—mine in the AAF, Armored Corp, and Cavalry and Mathe's in the Marine Corps. Mathe's dad flew for the Corps and didn't make it back to his home, wife, and baby—to their farm in Pennsylvania. Mathe didn't remember him—he was too little. His mom didn't tell him much when he asked. Too much to say, maybe.

When Mathe first met my dad and saw all the war photos framed on the den wall, he thought Dad was God. He hung on his every word like it was gospel and was constantly asking him to talk about his wartime experiences. He'd give Mathe little bits and pieces and change the subject as fast as he could. It all seemed like some incredible adventure to our naive minds.

My mom kept scrapbooks of his military life—she was with him for some of it, and it just added even more fuel to my ambition to fly. We poured over those scrapbooks in awe—at the size of his B-29 and the men he flew with. His experience and vision loomed large in our eyes and stoked our fire to fly.

We pestered Dad to talk about his wartime experiences—constantly. We probed for any information whenever we could. We were relentless and just kept asking. He continued to look away from us or disregarded our questions in the hope we would drop the interrogation. Was it the "loose lips sink ships" hangover?

One rainy day, our endless questions broke the dam.

Dad seemed to understand finally that we just had to know. Sitting on the floor in the den, he began to talk—much more than ever before—about his wartime survival.

He had never told us why he didn't fly after the war even though he had command "heavy time," as a pilot in the biggest airplane of its day. We had asked him a million times, but it became obvious after what he told us that day.

He started his story with, "Your mother and I"—like they were a team during the war years, and you know they were. To survive the uncertainty of those times must have been very scary. They needed each other.

He stared at us for a while with a faraway look in his eyes. I think he knew our futures before we did. He took us to his former world and the many aircraft he had flown and some of the fun and pain associated with each.

He went back to 1944—and we went with him.

"Boys, what I'm about to tell you happened some time ago and I have forgotten some parts on purpose. No one should have to go through it or hear about it ever again. I share this with you just one time because I think you are ready and strong enough to understand."

Dad rarely smoked, but today he brought out a pipe and lit it. It was peculiar to me to watch the smoke curl around his head as he drew in the smoky tobacco flavored smoke and released it between the following words. This was slowly becoming an event to relish and Mathe and I were all ears.

"It's a story about some brave men—my B-29 crew. You might have met a few. Some have stopped by for our reunions and Fourth of July celebrations. We been tasked with bombing the home islands of Japan, and our flight was comprised of B-29 bombers flying from our home base in Piardoba, India—what a place, but that is a whole other story.

My crew was solid, professional—friends who would do anything for each other regardless of rank. They were as tight as a tactical flight crew could be. In the beginning, they loved their jobs and were good at them—they loved airplanes, and the B-29 we flew was amazing. Once we got into the air, most of our everyday living concerns melted away until we were over the target or the enemy showed up. But, in time, the never-ending deaths of other crew members took us over. It brought fear and dysfunction as it burrowed deeper into our souls.

They were not much older than both of you. You guys will be in college soon. Most of my crew never had the chance to go—with the war and all. But, they were as smart and driven as both of you. And most of all, they wanted to live past the crucible of war and have real lives—full and long."

He interjected. "I know both of you will lead a serious life not letting sloppiness slip in—right?" he added with a smile. "So, stay committed to your dreams, your passions—never surrender them. I see a warrior in each of you that will never let you give up—wherever your futures take you. So do whatever it takes to achieve your goals, and if it is aviation, so be it."

"You will never be better or worse than the guys in this story. They all had their problems but never let their problems affect their duties—they used those problems as fuel."

With his next words, Dad honed in on Mathe, his second son—as their eyes met. "Try to let go of the past. It's hard but try. It will only mess up your future. Then turn those obstacles into opportunities. It is out there for both of you—so go get it," he said.

"Mathe, I know you've got some problems at home, but we don't need to talk about that right now. I'm here, though, if you ever want to talk."

I looked at Mathe's angry, rebellious, embarrassed expression. He was always at our house and never invited anyone to his. His mom was a heartbreaking embarrassment, seriously stifling his emotional growth. I think Mathe reminded Dad of some of his war buddies—feisty, always getting into fights, a swashbuckling, authority-challenging maverick. He was volcanic but smart as hell.

"Mathe, you can be a pain in the ass sometimes, but I get it," Dad said. "You are smart and reckless in a controlled sort of way—kind of like some of the guys in my crew. Finn tells me that you have had to work hard for everything you've achieved."

"The military just might be your answer—with the imprint of an officer and a gentleman stamped all over you. You are intelligent, independent, and tough but with a bit of irreverent bravado." I looked over and could see Mathe slowly melt from dad's words—with the recognition that someone cared about him.

"Finn, my son, you are spoiled. You seem to lack inner direction and constantly push boundaries to the nth degree. You just need to grow up. You are smart and happy-go-lucky with an edge of goofiness—but ferocious underneath it all. A military flight program, if you choose it, will bring out the best in you. Copious amounts of discipline will do wonders for you."

I turned to Mathe and said, "What the hell does copious mean?" Mathe meekly smiled back and didn't answer. It was now obvious that Dad accepted Mathe as a major player in my life—and wanted the best for both of us.

Dad gave us that stare and must have been thinking: *Both these guys questioned authority, mine and others, and it could become a problem for them in the military if they could not grow to see the bigger picture in the uniform they might someday wear. These two boys in their rough-edged status as teenagers strike a balance, in stressful situations, between remaining passive and displaying reckless behavior that could get them into trouble.*

What I didn't know about Dad, until many years later, was that he was selected as General Smith's aide while in India. This assignment gave him more freedom than most pilots until the day he flew Smith's B-25 at a low level, in a dust up, over the field at Piardoba. This story relayed to me by mom gave me a whole new outlook on my pop's war time shenanigans.

Eight: 'Our Gal' Puts on Her Clothes

WWII Reflections – David Finley
"Sing, Sing, Sing" – Benny Goodman

The smoke from Dad's pipe now filled the room and his energy seemed to increase as he recounted each memory as if it was yesterday. I guess flying the biggest bomber in the country in the day was beyond exciting and I could tell that flying meant more to him than I ever realized. I kept trying to visualize what it must have been like with that type of responsibility for his crew and the big bomber as his words now increased in pace as his excitement grew.

"Boys, whenever I hear you guys play 'Beautiful Girl' I can't help but recall another girl. We called her 'Our Gal' and she was painted on the side of our B-29 bomber. We cherished her and patted her down before each mission—when no one else was looking. She was our good luck talisman every time we crawled into her," Dad said.

"Nose art, those half-naked ladies painted on the side of our bombers, became very important to the crews—the more personal, intimate, and irreverent the better. We were young—the oldest of us twenty-four. Something a bit shocking might cause our enemy to pause in his pursuit of shooting down our plane. Themes ran from saucy to cartoons/caricatures to famous people. What the hell—the more garish the better. If it relieved some tension, let it rip. It was a lot of fun, and every man thought he was an artist.

'Our Gal' represented a crewman's girlfriend or wife or the dream of one. She was painted on the side of our B-29—lots of curves, free of clothing. We swore her loins and bountiful breasts heaved with expectation when we passed through the huge underside of the airplane. No one else was allowed to touch her except my crew.

When one of the crew's wives received a letter with a picture of 'Our Gal' on the side of our plane, she was so embarrassed that she decided to edit the picture herself. She sent the revision back to her husband in the hope that the boys would help her get dressed.

While taxiing out and waiting for our turn to take off, we caught the stares and the ogles from other aircraft aircrew members faces smiling behind their portholes and plexiglass cockpit windows. She was a real beauty and they knew it. 'Our Gal' was ours and there to protect on each mission and it was a sad day when we had to put her clothes back on.

Our B-29 was known for its ability to hit targets more than three thousand miles distant—approaching a span from New York to Paris. It took 85 officers and 73 enlisted personnel to support originally a 14-man aircrew to keep the B-29 combat airworthy.

So, let me tell you about one particular mission. It had been a good day. All targets were destroyed and we had not lost anyone. We were on our way home on our first leg to Tinian.

Doc, our pilot, with me as copilot, and our crew of 10 had reached our homeward-bound service ceiling of Fl300 (30,000 feet), with engines in sync and reading the required RPMs for max cruise speed on our homeward-bound leg. Doc had pressurized the airplane and we settled in for the long trip, RTB (return to base), with little expectation of additional combat at our altitude. But you never knew for sure—so we kept the edge. Suddenly, everything changed.

The Japanese had been taking a real pasting from our strikes deep into their home islands for the last few weeks. Out of nowhere, we were gunned—and good. They must have needed some payback. A Zeke fighter? We weren't sure."

* * *

Our side gunner, Jim Talbert, told it this way:
'The shock of the attack cleared my head enough to focus on the shell damage to the interior of our B-29. Our side viewing blister was in shreds, and there was a second gaping hole in the side of the airplane. Peering through the decompression frost—I groped for support in my tilted and a rapidly increasing painful world—for an escape route out of the rear of our B-29. I had to get out.

I could see Luke, our radio operator, from the front of the airplane—crumpled, mumbling, and plastered against the rear bulkhead. But where was Dan, our radar operator? I asked myself what was Luke doing back here.

My first step brought me crashing down as I slid through the pool of red at my feet. Peering through the windy condensation and flying electrical sparks of our wounded bird, I recognized Jimmy, our other side gunner. His body was dangling from his arm, which was wrapped around what was left of a section of aircraft electrical cable. He was unconscious against the airframe. It looked like he had secured himself by wrapping his arm around a cable, to keep from being sucked out of the airplane. He had taken the full force of the shell that had punctured the airplane's rear pressure vessel.

Lieutenant, the last thing I remembered was the ball of flame hanging in the air before my eyes and the smell of exploded gunpowder and calling Doc for help before going totally out—not from Gs but my injuries and lack of oxygen.'

* * *

"While all this was going on in the rear of the aircraft, Doc—our command pilot for this mission—leaned over to me. He shouted, 'Dave, that call from Jim is not good. They are in trouble and I still haven't heard from Luke. I sent him back 10 minutes ago!' "The rapid loss of pressure in the rear of the airplane gave me an early warning before I heard our gunners cry for help.

Doc ordered the initiation of the emergency depressurization procedure and notified the crew. He threw the bomber immediately into a steep left bank—and pushed Our Gal's nose over while we grabbed our O2 masks. I told our crew to keep an eye out for any Japanese fighters—like the one that got us.

Andy, our flight engineer, started to report his assessment of our situation from his instrument readings. Andy began closing the cabin air valves and opening the cabin pressure relief valve.

The cabin can be quickly depressurized by pulling either of the two emergency cabin pressure release handles—the one that read RESTRICTED—on the airplane commander's control stand and the starboard sidewall of the rear pressure compartment.

We were coming down from altitude hard, and without a word from Luke, Doc ordered me back to the rear of the airplane. I would be his eyes, and I awkwardly pulled myself along the tunnel, to the rear of the airplane, with a partially attached O2 mask, juggling an A-4 O2 [four to six minutes of air] bottle. This was not good.

Doc had given me a clue with his order for the full depressurization of our B-29. Were we on fire or preparing to abandon ship?

I pulled myself out of the tube into the rear of the plane and tried to steady myself on the slippery, windblown, blood-soaked deck. The fuselage was dyed with gore from my boys, Luke and "Tilly," who lay in disarray on the floor with Jimmy hanging by one arm from an electrical cable on the side of the airplane. I jumped to their needs and got their masks positioned and oxygen flowing. I did what I could but I needed help. They needed to say alive!

I glanced at the gaping holes through the fuselage and outside at the horizon line that was tilting as Doc continued his pushover to increase the angle of attack for our dive to breathable air. Close to 45 degrees now but Doc seemed to be in control—'Our Gal' was rock steady even with two new gaping holes driven into her side. Three hundred knots, the B-29's never-exceed speed, kept ringing in my ears.

Good girl, you can take it! I yelled in between Doc's calls of, 'Lieutenant, what the hell is going on back there? Report!'

While trying to find the medical kit, my attention became fixated on the partially severed control cables on the inside of the fuselage. *How had my crew survived this explosion?* I asked myself. I thought it was only a matter of time before the cables failed and we all had to leave. I had to move fast to save my crew.

I evaluated Jimmy, our side gunner, and Luke, our radio operator. They were in bad shape. I did not want to think about who might have been sucked out of the airplane as I searched for Dan, our radar operator. He was just not where he was supposed to be.

My fingers suddenly began to tingle and my vision started to tunnel—as my A-4 O2 bottle had run out. *Find another or plug into the ship's main O2 lines*, I told myself—which I did.

Got to report to Doc. Finding the ship's throat mic link, I plugged in. Squeezing the mic against my throat, I yelled, Doc, the rear compartment is a mess. There are two gaping holes in the fuselage, the blister has disintegrated, and our control cables are in bad shape—hanging by a thread. Jimmy is in bad shape too. I need to attend to their wounds. Tilly, our other side gunner, is coming around, but I can't find Dan. I'll get back to you after I sort this out.

Luke lay crumpled against the rear compartment bulkhead—his lights were on but nobody was home. He didn't have the kind of injuries associated with the explosive round through the side of the aircraft. His legs and arms akimbo told me he was broken up pretty bad. He had lots of bloodstains from assorted cuts. Being out of his normal crew position upfront, at the wrong time, told me he was probably pulling himself through the tube that separated the front from the back of the airplane at the moment of decompression as I remembered the emergency procedure that had been drilled into us —

Stay out of the tunnel as much as possible. If you are in there and pressure is lost suddenly, you may be shot out like a cork."

* * *

Luke later told me:

'You know, Lieutenant, I don't remember much except for flying across the back end of the ship and hitting the bulkhead after the decompression. I was the cork in the bottle. I feel really bad about Dan.'

* * *

"I then untangled Jimmy's body and lowered him to the floor. I noticed his searing back wounds, which had shredded his flight suit and parachute harness. He was out.

Safety training kicked in and I remembered: If a man is unconscious or nearly so from anoxia [lack of oxygen], get a mask on him that works and connect it to a working regulator. Turn the emergency valve to 'ON' until he recovers. In the case of serious wounds of any kind, see that the man gets pure oxygen regardless of altitude. I again reached each man's mask/connections, confirmed they were tightened down, and confirmed free flow on each valve.

Looking at the hole in the side of the fuselage, my first thought was that I didn't think the Japanese had a fighter that could reach our altitude of 30,000 feet and that the damage had to be ground fire. I refocused again and remembered: If a man is unconscious or nearly so, STOP THE BLEEDING, SUSTAIN BREATHING, PREVENT SHOCK, RELIEVE PAIN, AND PREVENT/RESTRICT WOUND INFECTION.

Tilly, our other side gunner, was showing signs of anoxia with rambling comments and periodic uncontrolled emotional displays—uncontrolled yelling. But, he was coming back to life and I was hopeful.

I applied small Carlisle bandages tightly against each man's wounds to stop their bleeding. Luke's compound fractures were bleeding heavily, and even my initial firm pressure did not stop the blood loss. As I applied tourniquets above the wounds, his bleeding slowed. I turned into a sulfa powder fairy, sprinkling each man's wounds while applying dressings. A fair amount of sulfa stuck to each wound, but the majority was whisked away in the windy maelstrom flowing through our holed-out ship.

Though gravely wounded, Jimmy was now talking coherently as he scratched shell fragments out of his face, neck, and shoulder. The bleeding from the compound fracture in his arm and a deep gash in his right thigh had slowed significantly.

I then reported back to Doc again: "Tilley, Jimmy, and Luke seem to be coming around, but I have not had a chance to check on Bill, our rear gunner. I think Dan was blown out of the airplane and will confirm when I get to Freddy in the rear."

* * *

I took a look a glance over at Mathe, his mouth hung open in horror as we listened. He caught my cringe as Dad continued to describe the horror of this scene. I wondered if I could face this scene with the courage that Dad had displayed. Could I suck it up and face my fears?

* * *

"Jimmy Lyann, our side gunner, relayed his story to me after the flight in the hospital post-op debrief—more than a week later:

'It happened so fast, Lieutenant. The side of the airplane just exploded right after the side blister blew out. I was talking with Dan over a candy bar and he was blown against the partially disintegrating side blister. I think I saw Luke hurtle past me as I grabbed for Dan, but with the rapid decompression, I couldn't be certain. I heard a loud crash and everything was flying toward the openings. God, it was scary.

Dan was yelling and screaming and I grabbed some cable on the side of the airplane to steady myself and was holding onto him for dear life as his body slowly got sucked into the airstream. I couldn't hold him and he couldn't hold on to me. I kept yelling for help but no one came—and now I know why. It was terrible. I guess I passed out. I don't remember much else after that.

In one coherent moment, I thought I was going to die. I didn't want to die yet I wasn't afraid of it either after the missions we had been through. I went from feeling sadness for those who might morn my loss to pure rage.

My injuries didn't hurt right off the bat but I had a really funny taste in my mouth and the pain steadily grew. I felt a growing need to sleep, which I fought off tooth and nail—to stay alive. I thought of my wife and my little girl, Beth. The pain and you being there helped me focus on staying alive and the desire to not give up. Thanks, Lieutenant.'

* * *

"Well, boys, Doc wrestled the big bomber home, but 'Our Gal' was in bad shape—like her crew. She wouldn't fly for a while so we were assigned a new ride. The loss of Dan hurt, but we all tried to adjust to it with a new sense of purpose to survive.

We named our new mount 'Starduster' in Dan's remembrance and welcomed our reassigned crew members, who filled in for those healing and lost."

Nine: Surviving the Hump

WWII Reflections – David Finley
"Moonlight Serenade" – Glenn Miller

Dad continued to tell us his story.

"You know, boys, we met soldiers from many countries, but my memory of our British military officers in India remains very positive.

The officers that we dealt with daily were very fluent in the region's cultures and customs. They had an orientation and spirit about the execution of the war that I liked. They were kindred spirits with a balance, style, and aggressive approach to carrying out their operations. It seemed as if they were truly in tune with the positive outcome that would be theirs, and they celebrated that day in and day out in battle and the officers' club each night.

Their approach to this war helped me broaden my view of another way to get through this. They strengthened my mindset and inner resolve daily.

The B-29 was armed with an assorted array of weapons and technology so it could defend itself against attacks. Mounted on the top near the cockpit was a radio or electronically controlled turret with four-barreled .50-caliber machine guns. A similar turret was mounted on the bottom of the plane under the cockpit and another was located near the tail of the plane. The tail and side gunners had a .30-caliber or .50-caliber weapon depending upon the plane.

After a particularly hairy mission over Yawata, Staff Sergeant Freddy Patterson, a tail gunner, came to me with an idea to try to put an end to the severe rear attacks we had been having by the echelons of Zeros that swept through his quadrant.

'Let's put a large broomstick out the rear of the airplane with a can on the end poked full of holes. It will look like a howitzer and should scare the hell out of the Japs. I'll still be able to shoot with the .50s on either side. What do you think?'

On the next mission, there were fewer attacks from the rear. I quietly chuckled as others in the formation started to quiz us on how they could get their hands on the new armament for their aircraft. Even so, while fighter attacks were bad, you could at least shoot back. I think it was the anti-aircraft fire was the most worrisome.

You know, boys, I couldn't end our discussion today if I didn't talk about one fateful fuel resupply mission deep into China from our base in northern India—over The Hump. We were again flying in the China Burma Theater with the 20th Air Corps in 1944.

It all started with a call from our flight engineer.

First Lieutenant Art Toomey yelled over the inter-phone, 'Doc, our No. 4 is showing a drop in oil pressure and the cylinder head temperature is rising.

Keep an eye on it, Art, and let me know if your numbers go further south,' Captain Doc Wessel, our pilot, replied.'

As the flight's co-pilot, I knew that the B-29's engines had bugs and created problems for many other aircrews stationed out of Piardoba, India. For some, these problems had bad outcomes. We were often overloaded to 140,000 to 160,000 pounds gross weight, causing the engines to overheat. Part of the crew's response was to watch the engines during the long flights so that at the first sign of overheating or fire, countermeasures could be taken.

I often wondered what my boys were thinking about as we droned on into the night—bugs and all. Eighteen hours of B-29 flight time, per mission, gave all of us a lot of time to think about family and finding ourselves. Many men were pondering a civilian career or continued peacetime service and the chance to marry someone special or the arrival of a new son or daughter.

As the flight droned on I remember scratching my nose— remembering a past open cockpit flight. To this day when it gets cold out, my nose, enlarged from being frozen in an open cockpit PT-19 primary trainer, still turns half white and half red—and I mean right up to the middle—one of the strangest sights you can imagine.

I would rather be flying than not, even though we had everything at 'Little America Piardoba'—except for the things I wanted, of course. If you weren't killing time, you were flying, and the former was painful as you watched your life pass by.

The military service had given and taken away much in each crewman's life. Of course, for many, it was the loss of friends that cut the deepest. We mourned those who didn't return in very personal ways.

First, the loss of Lieutenant Edward Pearcel, a football star from Flint Northern and a three-year letter winner at Michigan State, on a mountainside in French Morocco. Then, First Lieutenant Charles Mill, MSU halfback, piloting a Liberator over France, failed to return. Pearcel, Mill, and I all had remained together through 14 transfers to camps and bases, moving from the Cavalry to the Armed Forces and then to the Air Force. We all received our wings together following the same path. These men were also drinking buddies, roommates with their crews and squadrons. I knew them and they knew me better than most. When they died they often just didn't go quietly by themselves. Whole crews, at one time—whole barracks—just gone.

Our pilot training was a strain and the constant movement from base to base a challenge. Our wives made the best of each posting and we tried to keep each other's spirits up. Simple pleasures were the name of the game and we made our own.

The heat in Hayes, Kansas, was oppressive so Chuck, Eddie, and I went into town and purchased a block of ice and borrowed a fan. We sat with our wives in the 'Country Club,' a converted farmhouse attic, and laughed at our new air-conditioned digs.

Several days later we suited up for a training flight and instead of 11 crew members, 22 boarded our B-17. Each was in full flight leathers with goggles, and we were stuffed into every corner of the aircraft as we climbed out of Walker Field to a much higher altitude.

Giggles coming from some of the strangest places—a flying love boat—for each crew member had brought his wife or girlfriend.

Finn, believe it or not, your mom took the yoke and horsed the big bomber around the sky. Billy Ann now a bomber pilot? Who would have thought? Hopefully, this experience might make up for all the waiting she would have to endure during my tour.

Later, when I heard that Billy was attending the Michigan-Ohio State football game, we promptly planned a cross-country flight direct to Columbus with a flyover that dusted the stadium. Billy told me about the wide-eyed crowd and how our buzz job caused Ohio State to fumble on an important drive—mission complete!"

Yes, fellas, all that time in the seat gives a guy lots of time to think and remember. My mind wandered off to my days at Culver Military

Academy. It was great preparation for my military career, but I loved the horses and men in Culver's Black Horse Troop. It was a proud moment for our troop participating in the Philadelphia Thanksgiving Day Parade.

The pride we took in taking care of our horses, tack, and uniforms, which were on display that November day in 1938. Jumping competitions at school allowed us to explore the true bond between our horses and a way to excel at our ability and as a team. My work with the border patrol in Tucson proved to be a natural extension of these proud days at Culver Military Academy.

I was a horseman all right, yet in time I would come to understand that the pragmatic needs of the service came first over my love for these great animals. Many horses ridden for the border patrol, over time, did not measure up to military standards and had to be dispatched.

It was painful to watch sergeants who truly loved their animals, .45 in hand and lowered heads, approach the company stable. They had worked with each for years and were beyond grief to have to carry out the order. I could not watch them in their pain so I took over their jobs to save them from this misery. We had explored every avenue to save these creatures but the service would not relent. All I can say is that it was very quick for the ponies but left a longtime scar that still has not healed.

Technology finally caught up with us and the Army replaced our horses with tanks. Ed, Chuck, and I wanted no part of that army and immediately transferred to the Air Corps."

Ten: Starduster's Struggle

WWII Reflections – David Finley
"Don't Sit Under the Apple Tree" – Glenn Miller

"Staff Sergeant James Lyann, our right gunner, yelled over the inter-phone, 'Doc, you know that hot engine—No. 4? Well, she's smoking now.'

Here we go, I thought, as Doc told James to keep an eye out for flames and First Lieutenant Art Toomey, flight engineer, to get on the gauges and monitor engine performance, fuel flow, and his emergency checklist—everything!

No. 4's timing could not have been worse. We were at 34,000 feet over the Himalayas. This was not a bombing mission but a cargo flight—no hotbeds of Jap resistance today. We carried eight rubberized fuel tanks secured in the bomb racks, 2,900 gallons to offload after 13 more hours of flight direct to our advanced base in the Cheng Tu Valley—in preparation for the final push to finish off Japan's homeland.

We were a long way from home and that's a lot of fuel. A possible engine fire was now more frightening than being shot at over Kyushu and Yokohama.

I looked over at Doc, who was quietly concentrating on his next task. He was going through his emergency procedures and options while descending and reversing course—in case the worst happened. He knew 11 crew members and two passengers were counting on his life-or-death decisions. Doc told me to take the yoke, and I flew on our new heading. I kept an eye on No. 4 while probing Art for engine performance numbers and asking for constant updates from our engine eyes in the back. No. 4 was losing power and we smelled gas fumes in the front of the aircraft.

With sudden dramatic yaw to the right, Technical Sergeant Al Hess, our senior gunner, yelled, 'We've got thick black smoke coming out of No. 4 now.'

Quickly, I turned to confirm our problem child on the starboard wing. Doc gave me that look and I nodded confirmation of the reality of our problem. Our converted B-29 tanker was now in real trouble.

Doc quickly reduced power. The power reduction had reduced the volume of smoke, but within ten minutes a large column of oil and smoke suddenly streamed out of the upper nacelle. Staff Sergeant Dan Cartier, our radio operator, went to the forward bomb bay to investigate the gas fumes while Doc agitated over the possibility of fumes saturating the plane.

'Fire coming out of No. 4,' Al yelled. 'The flames are growing.'

Suddenly, there was a second shudder and Art looked at the engine instruments and notified us that the MAPs/RPMs on engine No. 4 were falling fast.

Doc called for Art to open the cowl flaps 15 degrees, and if that didn't put the fire out, to use both engine fire extinguishers.

In the process, Doc continued his descent while requesting confirmation of our heading to Piardoba from our navigator, First

Lieutenant Walt Russo. Art, James, and I all looked back at the engine. It was still ablaze and burning the upper and left side of the nacelle even after the extinguishers had been used. Not good!

The engine then shook violently again. To minimize drag on the dead No. 4, Doc told Art to feather the engine to minimize drag—turn the propeller blades parallel to the wind and stop the propeller's rotation. Because the propeller kept windmilling, it increased the drag and required Doc to use higher power settings to lift the dead wing and minimize the right yawing moment. The fire continued to burn furiously and Doc made the decision to leave the airplane.

He ordered all crew members to bail out.

After leveling us at 7,500 feet, Doc dropped the landing gear and opened the bomb bay doors. This slowed 'Starduster' down while we unhooked flak vests, unplugged com links, donned parachutes, grabbed what we could, and found our way to our respective exits.

I thought about my pilot hatch, jettisonable overhead window for a moment but found my way to the nose wheel well. Ed Helm, bombardier, crawled up through the crew compartment and met Al Hess and me over the nose wheel hatch. Len unlatched the hatch, and Ed exited quickly followed by Len. I turned and looked for Doc to follow and wondered what was holding him in the cockpit. Although the bomber was in bad shape, it was stable. Doc must have been holding the aircraft level so we could get out. I jumped and followed my crew toward the cloud layer below.

Tail gunner Freddy Paterson, side gunners Dick Lynch and James Lyann, and our two passengers leaped through the open bomb bay doors.

Little did we know that just as we exited the aircraft—to become official Caterpillar Club members—Art Tomey, our engineer, reported that the engine fire had gone out. The bailout was immediately stopped. It was now up to radio operator Dan Cartier, navigator Walt Russo, flight engineer Art Toomey, and pilot Doc Wessel to get 'Starduster' home.

We passed through a thin cloud layer with good open chutes and descended toward the largest lake I think I had ever seen in China. We had jumped without life vests—great! Who needs life vests for an overland mission? The cloud moisture we were falling through was like a slap in the face as I strained to find my widely dispersed descending crew.

I loosened the chute harness and had one leg unstrapped when I hit the water. The jungle survival kit floated free to the surface and I followed it. I was grateful that it floated. It kept me on the surface and supported my efforts to swim. No one else had landed near me. I swam about two hundred yards, calling several times. A native boatman ignored me as I clung to a bamboo pole sticking up in the water. After much hesitation to pick me up, their boat came alongside and hauled me in. We searched the area for quite a while and pulled chutes in. They were all empty. Ed and Al were waiting for us when I reached the island shore. But where was the rest of the crew? We were concerned for their safety but needed to find a way home and stay out of the hands of the Japanese.

Onshore, the Chinese natives served us tea and local food, and 12 hours later we were taken to Sunamganu. A British officer met us and offered to send a wire to Sylhet, the closest base to notify of our survival and location.

A final C-47 ride got us into Calcutta and then by train to Piardoba—18 days later. The concern for our missing crew members grew. No one seemed to know anything about them.

When I was finally reunited with Doc, he gave me the rest of the story.

Doc continued on course to Piardoba but was unable to maintain altitude because the runaway prop would not feather. He also did not jettison the bomb bay tanks because of his fear of spilling gas. A fire onboard could result in an explosion. His decision was compounded by the feeling that opening the bomb bay doors at such a low altitude would drop the airspeed below stall speed. It became very apparent that it would be impossible to reach Piardoba so Doc asked Walt for a heading for Kurmitola. When he could not hold altitude, he decided to ditch the aircraft (B-29 number 43-6263) 40 miles north-northeast of Kurmitola into a lake that lay directly on his course.

Dan Cartier, radio operator, Walt Russo, navigator, and Art Toomey, flight engineer, were on board with Doc as he flew 'Starduster" into the lake. She rose over a tree line before making initial lake contact in some bull rushes. There was no bounce nor any sudden jerking but just decisive slowing down as the aircraft sank into the lake. With strong gas fumes and water pouring in, everyone rapidly exited. They piled into the two remaining life rafts, thankful that no one was injured, and paddled to shore. Upon meeting some friendlies, they were fed and directed to the local police station for their negotiated journey back to Piardoba.

This is when we learned that three crew members lost their lives by drowning. The bodies of Staff Sergeant Sid Islet and Staff Sergeant Dick Lynch were recovered. Nothing was ever heard from Staff Sergeant Leonard Anderson. It is presumed that he drowned since fellow crew members report that he didn't know how to swim. We were all saddened to lose these guys.

Doc mentioned to me in passing that he ordered 'Starduster' destroyed: 'Dave, there was just too much valuable hardware in that bomber,' he said. 'It took two B-25 bomb runs, using 100-pound bombs, and a demolition crew to finish the job.'

We continued our missions for another four months until I received orders to return to the United States via a cross-country flight—Calcutta, Karachi, Abadan, Cairo, Tripoli, Casa Blanca, Dakar, Natal, Belem, British Guiana, Puerto Rico, and finally our destination in Miami.

I had survived! And I am grateful for that. Our family and friends and my new baby son welcomed me home.

And now you guys. Most of all I want you two to remember the most important lesson you can take from these experiences.

Do not believe in the glory of war. It is a myth—hear me!"

I looked at Dad as the air slowly drained out of his balloon and thought I understood a little of his pain. A glance and a smile at Mathe told me that we were just immature enough to not give up on our dream.

Glory or not—we decided it was our decision to experience and decide for ourselves. I knew that war would test us and that I would most likely lead with my heart more so than Mathe leading with his spear.

Eleven: Commitments

"Don't Get Sloppy with Your Lives."
"Suzie Q" – Creedence Clearwater Revival
"Midnight Rider" – Allman Brothers

1962

Even though Mathe was a U of M student, we welcomed his frequent visits and his eventual transfer to our fraternity house—in East Lansing. At the time, Ann Arbor was a hotbed of sit-ins, riots, and even bombings—antiwar all the way. We welcomed our brother and he found something he could not find on the U of M campus as he socialized and studied as a Spartan rather than a Wolverine. We all thought it was really the caliber of the females on campus that was the draw. Besides, Rusty was here.

The stars were aligned as Mathe, James, and I volunteered to fly for the Marine Corps our sophomore year and were admitted into the Marine Platoon Leaders Class Aviation (PLCA) program. The draft was irrelevant—WE WERE COMMITTED. At least I thought we were all on board with this decision.

James was 5'5" tall with little or no observable academic, athletic, or social skills. But, he was a total nut job and a lot of fun to be around if you wanted to have some irresponsible entertainment. We were all surprised that with his trust fund-baby background of spoiled ostentation that he would ever consent to join the Marine Corps. It was only a matter of time before his happy go lucky immature ways finally must have come to grips with the reality of our joint decision to join the Corps.

Several weeks later over a beer, James blurted out, "You know, I don't know if I necessarily believe in this war."

I saw Mathe's jaw drop and looked back at James. "What are you talking about—I thought we all agreed to enlist? You don't really have a choice now that we all are in—right?"

"Well, you see, I didn't enlist as we all discussed a month ago," James mumbled, as he stared off into space and gave me his goofy weak-ass grin, which told me he meant it. "Look, you guys, I'm not going with you—I gotta be truthful with you—I'm looking for a way out of the draft.

"You know we have had a lot of fun in college, but I can't abide by this military shit. I found a doctor who has written a letter to the draft board drawing attention to my ulcerous condition—so I can get out of the military. It's better than getting married while we're here. Besides, I have good friends who are SDS members and have been listening to their ways to beat the draft."

And for some reason, the words *lefty, liberal, coward* popped into my head simultaneously. A political science class flashback or a new vision of James sitting in front of me—I wasn't sure? I immediately dismissed these visions, as my rage rose.

"James, are you kidding us?" Mathe piped.

"No, I'm holding firm on this one—I'm not going. You can fuck the Marine Corps. Most everyone except you guys are protesting the war and looking for an escape anyway."

"WTF, James, I thought we were all in this together—the three of us. All of us are committed to going into the Corps and flying in Vietnam—we're on the line with our lives," I blurted out as we alternated from staring at the floor to glaring at him. "Are you afraid, James—don't like the government and its policies? What is it? Tell us."

For once in his life, James had opened up as our palatable hostility increased. Mathe's eyes hardened with seriousness and he yelled, "Are you a coward?"

Even so, I detected no certitude in James attitude or statement. He seemed to be speaking the party line without having given it much thought. Oh well, just James, I thought and started to dig in—peppering him to get at his truth.

OK, James, maybe you're worried about getting killed—afraid to fight for your country? I thought.

"Any worrying thoughts about the government lying to us, or misleading us?" I asked. *Maybe it was the chic thing to say and do—it seems everybody is bitching about the times and the war and so James followed. I wondered: Besides, there are really cute SDS coeds.*

"James, do you think the war is immoral? You have found an excuse not to serve as a lot of others. Do you think the draft process is corrupt? You know the draft board can be bought—is that it? Do you have any beliefs you will die for? Why are you against the war?"

James just sat there trying to collect a justification for his behavior while we drilled him.

I looked over at that hangdog look on James' face and realized: James was never passionate and fierce about much—except for his hedonistic drives. As I looked back, he just didn't have the social and political rage to join those who opposed the perceived injustices of our society. He was not severe or authentic—just too cautious for me to believe him.

So I hit him with the most absurd things I could think of.

"James, are you going to get married to evade the draft? Are you irritated because you think the man is oppressive and just screwing over the poor in this war? What is it, James?"

With an exasperated look, James just walked away from the conversation—*shrinking from the real truths of our times for his convenience.* Mathe and I looked at each other, not without concern for James, and realized we were back to two—just like in the beginning—and so we studied and partied on through our time left at MSU. We were pissed that our bond had been broken—possibly forever.

From that day forward Mathe and I continued to find ways to convince James to change his decision. But, he slowly melted away into his tribe of resisters.

His didn't seem to be courageous enough to reach for the dream of Tall Air.

* * *

The Navy offered orientation flights with a Marine lieutenant to show off the airplane we would be flying in the near future. I was beyond excited to jump upfront while I asked him to put the airplane through its paces. I missed his devilish grin as he put me through what he knew to be a torture chamber flight for his fledgling pilot initiate.

After barrel rolls, nuclear pickles, aileron rolls, wingovers, simulated stadium strafing runs, and more, we landed. I should have kept my mouth shut when I asked the lieutenant to show me everything the T-34 could do.

Totally trashed, I stumbled out of the plane after the flight with the biggest shit-eating grin in East Lansing. I was also seriously sick to my stomach. But so excited about a future adventure in the air—Naval Air.

"Hey, candidate Finley, maybe you should reconsider your application and acceptance to fly for the Corps," the lieutenant called out. I gave him a lame smile as I tried to catch my breath and clean off the mess I had made on the wing of his airplane.

After puking a couple more times, I slunk back to my dorm room and took a short two-hour nap. Physically, I thought I had seen it all in my 21-year-old life, but I realized that anything that could so thoroughly wring me out had to be explored. This had been the best and worst day of my life. We had one more adventure before things got serious. A long-planned trip to Europe for spring break—traveling on BMW motorcycles to as many places as we could drive to in 14 days.

We'd stay in hostels throughout France, Germany, and Italy, camping when and wherever we could, maybe a party or two with some beautiful European girls—what an adventure! The money we made working odd jobs throughout the year would fund this trip—we didn't need much.

Little did I know there would be a serious price to pay for this last escapade before graduation. It was the best trip ever—a ribald adventure in youthful foolishness, wine, and female explorations.

Hostels provided the perfect way to see the continent on our motorcycles. The friendliness of the German girls our age was amazing—I guess the U.S. '60s "Love Generation" had moved to

Europe. We ate copious quantities of bread, cheese, fruit, salami, chocolate, and wine as we rode our way through Europe, laughing and conquering each new adventure.

It all passed so quickly, and before we knew it we were back in the fraternity, studying hard to get through our senior year. Well, one of us had to study more than the other.

Mathe became obsessed with climbing things—again. He'd continued our adventure by driving pitons into the outside brick wall of the fraternity house and roping in for his circumnavigation to show off his new mountaineering skills learned in the Italian mountains.

Yes, there were parties, a lot of them. They were laced with alcohol and didn't end until the wee morning hours. The fun never seemed to wear Mathe out. To impress the coeds Mathe would move around the room hanging from the ceiling moldings—by his fingers and nothing else.

At one particular party I remembr catching James yawning— either from party boredom or being overserved. He gave a nod and we both exited the room.

"James, let's take one more ride tonight—south of the campus. Get your bike," my beer-compromised voice slurred.

"You're on, Finn." James said. "But let's get Mathe." We couldn't find Mathe but suspected he had more on his mind as I passed the fogged-up windows of Rusty's car.

"Nah, not this time, Mathe," I mumbled smiling to myself—as steam seemed to pour out of the back seat window.

Hearing the distinct sound of a BMW motorcycle muffler, I hurried over to my matching BMW cycle and then pulled up beside James.

"Mathe won't be joining us tonight," I smirked and pointed to Rusty's car.

He understood, and with a grin from ear to ear gunned the BMW. I guess Mathe was finally learning how to communicate with Rusty.

James smiled as he pulled away and I followed. What a perfect fall night ride—a speed run with the freedom of the wind, a few beers, and the challenge of the darkness. *Nothing can hurt us tonight,* I thought. Our joyride didn't last long as James pulled away and I lost him in the darkness. Rather than follow, I turned back to our fraternity house.

I was brought to consciousness, around 3:30 a.m., by flashing lights flashing in the window and sirens blaring in the night. A police vehicle was parked in the back of the fraternity house. I looked over at James' empty bunk—not there. Was he in trouble?

I hurried outside and told the officer that I was with James earlier in the evening and had lost him in the night before I turned for the house. James loved speed and would race all or anything that challenged him.

The officer told me that they had found his body and battered motorcycle near the train tracks. I could not believe that he had died—hit by a train south of campus—an hour earlier.

The picture in my mind was clear: He probably had challenged the train—paralleled its course on the empty road beside the tracks to beat it to the crossroad intersection. He didn't make it and the engine took him out.

I didn't always agree with Mathe and, in fact, many times when I thought he was losing his shit, we tangled. Many of these times James was there to separate us—but not anymore. While I let Mathe know he could do better even when we didn't agree, we learned to accept our differences/his tirades—painful as they were. But, James and his ability to moderate our clashes would be severely missed, and his personality probably would have provided a welcome tonic to ease the pressure we would feel when we began flying in the next year.

The brothers and all who knew him were devastated. A great guy was gone. Little did I know that I would lose others in the career choice that Mathe and I had chosen. The pain of James passing stung for many years. Our three was now two. His goofy humor was sorely missed.

Fall turned into winter and Mathe and I became quieter. I had no idea what was going on in Mathe's head after the shock of James' death. We both studied a lot, didn't party as much—didn't want to. When I thought about all the stupid shit we had done when we were younger it amazed me we hadn't ended up like James. I really think his death prompted a need for us to value life a little more, for we finally realized it could be taken away in seconds.

With the coming of spring, life for us got a little brighter as competitive juices flowed in expectation of the upcoming lacrosse season. Mathe had been introduced to lacrosse in Pennsylvania and he took to it like a fish to water. He slowly broke me into the "Spirit of the Stick"—the essence of this rewarding and wonderful game. It did not take long for my blood to boil with the love and expectation that arose with each new season—almost like Spock's Vulcan *pon farr* excitement for those who were committed to the sport. Lacrosse offered a perfect outlet for a pair of aggressive misfits like us.

The most enjoyable times were spent on the lacrosse field actively engaging our opponents—which sometimes included spectators. It was a great release from our studies. Some games brought back memories of wrecking others on the middle school smear court. The score was important but the smashmouth physical contact and team camaraderie was the reason we loved the game. It gave the chips on our shoulders new meaning as we sparred with other players from the Big Ten,

Patriot League, and select Ohio schools. This was our preview of a different kind of conflict—real war.

Thinking of the MSU lacrosse daze, I'm still having a hard time wiping the smile off my face.

Oh, those away-game trips—smelly cars loaded with sticks hanging out windows, the unwashed stench of our uniforms, and beer breath that no amount of vehicle ventilation could fix. Even with all the camaraderie, there were high expectations for a chance to notch another win, in Spartan colors.

The Lehigh "mud bowl"—with a muddy field that covered our ankles seemed to piss us off—Lafayette sure paid the price the next day from our anger. It was amazing pulling into towns and the college coeds hearing that we were the opposing team—encouraging us to keep drinking more beer the night before so that their team might have an advantage the next day. We had to sleep in a small Ohio State fraternity house room before game day with a well-placed cat that continually crawled over our faces in the middle of the night to give us as little sleep as possible. Notre Dame was comprised of a nasty ball-thumbing bunch of football castoffs who made you keep your head up or you could lose it during the game. Denison offered a nice rowdy group of fans to chirp with and so much more—but a great coach and disciplined players.

The bench-clearing brawl with spectators was classic. So too was the cleat dance on the back of an opponent laying on the turf after getting clocked for making a bad decision to challenge one of our key defensemen. One New England college had a notorious Native American attackman who played without shoes. Our defenseman stepping on this barefooted attackman— quickly ended his game.

Over the years, we both developed a kind of streetfighter attitude—stretch or break the rules if it fit the time. We broke with traditions and rules in any and every way possible. The lacrosse field was ready-made for our shoulder chips. Don't get me wrong: We played the games straight, by the rules, but with added aggression that sometimes could not be reined in by ourselves—even after the games.

Scrappy adaptation and guts powered us through many uncomfortable situations, and we developed an attitude to be ready for conflict wherever we found it. And the more uncomfortable the situation, probably the better.

The postgame faces of strong, disciplined varsity teams that were completely dismantled by what they thought to be a bunch of undisciplined club rag tags was priceless—humorous memories to this day. An analogy might be the vision of the Stanford marching band coming onto the field at halftime football games right after the U of M marching band had completed their program. Stark style differences was an understatement—and a hilarious difference in approach to music entertainment. Stanford won hands down—just like we did. We got it done in our own style, which mystified many.

Nah, we didn't really party before games—maybe a loosener or two that continued into a ribald classic mess that just got better after the game. I think. Some of it is a bit fuzzy.

The Vietnam War was raging, and Mathe and I knew we had to get into this fight. The Marine Corps was waiting for us.

I was truly entertained by the attitudes of many of my generation—those who made the soft, easy choices or who valued their skins more than the rules that governed our great country. You know—peace and love with all its frivolity and attitudes reinforced by a copious dose of psychedelic drugs. I was sympathetic to their direction. How easy it would have been to join my liberal friends, but I knew our direction was right for me and important.

Maybe the thought of a Marine drill instructor (DI) beating the shit out of me in Officer Candidate School was a more noble alternative than a Chicago cop working me over in some '60s protest. Were we that desperate to prove our selves—to find our manhood? Republican or Democrat—I had a vague concept of the differences, but being Episcopal was good enough for me. My dad had some words to share, and I still remember what he said a few years earlier.

"OK, so I will tolerate your liberalness, but if your not staunchly conservative by the time your 30 we are going to have a discussion." Most kids got the same advice, but for most, it did not stick. His words kept ringing in my ears, *"Don't get sloppy with your lives or lose your goals and vision of your future."* He knew from experience that if we were still liberal by 30 we might be lost as useful tools to society and ourselves.

It took me many years to understand the disparity and truths about our two-party political system—more specifically the significant deviation from the standard or norms of our society by one in particular. It was an easy and obvious choice to make—for me at least. OK, socially liberal, but in all other factors of my life, staunchly conservative. Don't tell Dad.

As frivolous as it seemed, I felt I had more important things to do— the excitement of a different kind of experience in my life. I was disaffected by the temptations that followed most other students. I simply had done it already in high school, and it was time to move on.

A broken leg on a junior year ski trip kicked me off the lacrosse team and out of the Marine Corps. In the fall of my sophomore year, Mathe and I signed to fly for the Marine Corps and the compound fracture had compound consequences. Unable to join the Corps for summer camp, I promptly received a full honorable discharge. But, I found my way back into the Navy's flight program as an AOC (Aviation Officer Candidate). What the hell, just a uniform change. If it allowed me to fly a military jet, I was OK with it. Mathe stayed with the Marines—a perfect fit.

As I look back at our youthful antics, who would have thought our acceptance into the "The NAV" (Navy) could ever be a reality. Our suburban irresponsibility went beyond anything imaginable by most: group skinny-dips at night around the neighborhood; fistfights in local drive-ins and dance halls against more seasoned greasy-haired, stilleto-toed combatants who had little disposition to take our superfluous suburban jokes; seltzer bottle attacks on hitchhikers as we stopped at intersections and gave 'em what for; ski ticket and complete ID printing forgeries in the back of vans parked near local ski resorts; and garaging for beer were now things of the past.

It was strange how the Navy took us and turned our natural and sometimes irreverent instincts and drives into supporting a cause, a reason to live greater than ourselves. It changed us as officers and men. It demanded a total buy-in because it was hard, challenging, and sometimes painful to succeed under Navy rules that demanded everything we had and more. Our never-quit attitudes were now tested to the max and magnified to a whole new level by the challenge. It felt good, and we loved it.

The Set-Up

As the story is passed down, I'm sure every Marine drill instructor associated with training naval aviation officer candidates wished they had been there for my indoctrination to the Navy way. My recruiter sold me on the flight program and described how easy it would be.

"You will love it, Finn. It's just like a country club, and they pay you to fly," Gunny Abruzzo said.

I was hooked.

"So bring your tennis racket and golf clubs when you drive into Battalion One. Your gunnery sergeant will give you a good welcome and might even take you over for a beer before your training starts." *Yeah, right!*

But I bought it, I really did.

As I pulled into the front gate of the Pensacola Naval Air Station, the guard took one look at all the stuff in the open back seat of my car and smiled. He directed me to "Batt. One." I didn't understand why the base guards were chuckling to each other as I passed through the front gate, until an hour later.

"Just like a country club, Finn", kept ringing in my ears.

I was all smiles as I grabbed the heavy wooden doors of Battalion One and felt the awful fear of the unknown. Juggling the clubs, rackets, and much more, I met the ominous stare of a Marine drill instructor. I tried to shake his hand while juggling my soon-to-be past life in my arms. I smelled a raw harsh obedience emerging from the hallways. My new tribal lemming instincts took hold as the environment inside dictated an unknown and more severe atmosphere.

The last thing I remember of that day, after signing in, was continuously getting my ass kicked both verbally and physically. I pushed the *this-is-a-mistake* thought out of my mind and tried not to show too much fear. I just took it. I was now "The Target," and the drill instructors each took their best shots. The shunning continued for 10 weeks. I wanted to succeed badly and was continually being told I was a fuck-up and didn't measure up. Each barb the bull's-eye, me, daily, in their drive to cull me from the ranks of aviation officer candidates. I was astonished by the DI's frenzied behavior in the first ten weeks. My hidden smile of disbelief dissolved into braced attention as the seriousness of failing drove me harder. Suck it up. I had to survive the first round or go home

Even though I felt I was different, I struggled to conform—and slowly become invisible. In lockstep, not willing to surrender, they took me apart piece by piece. They were very efficient in their drive to transform my civilian attitude to one in the Navy's flying brotherhood. I sucked it up and suffered the barbs in the hope of proving myself to my father's expectations.

Sure, the Navy had its traditions. They were steeped in history and inflexible, but I found a way to navigate the process and fly the Navy way—even though I at times had my doubts. I also knew Mathe must have been going thru the same crap.

Entry into the flight program and commissions were eventually achieved. Many thought it was like putting socks on a rooster, for both of us. We were now one Marine lieutenant and one Navy ensign— Mathe and I.

Were we really that two-headed coin—wearing different hats that would make the right decisions alone or together.

Yes, we both hung on to get winged. I know Mathe struggled too, in a different sort of way with the Marine Corps. It was new territory for both of us. As I tried to look into our futures, I realized that I might not see Mathe for a while for I would be assigned to sea duty and his assignment would most likely take him to a land-based Marine squadron.

As time passed and we grew with the service, I began to suspect there would come a day when our self-preservation, in this upside-down war, would come to blows with the command structure.

Warriors we were, but our true characters were separated from Navy rituals by our ingrained skeptical independence. It was the strength that could not be stripped away. We just didn't follow the rules very well—too independent to not question. The Navy just couldn't get us to turn that corner completely. It would probably come out in a face-to-face with one of our senior officers—and it did.

Twelve: Wives/Girlfriends

Maddy's Irreverent Tribe
"Under My Thumb" – Rolling Stones

1961-1969

At 14, girls were still a mystery to me. I had never learned to talk to them and was very uncomfortable around them.

I never knew what to say or how to start a conversation, but whatever magic occurs at that age took the shyness away. Gradually they became very interesting.

I had my eye on one in particular. Mathe, on the other hand, had his eye on 10, but I'll get into that later.

Maddy had grown up a lot! A blond ponytail that swung back and forth as she walked, a nice smile, and she seemed smart. And I was knocked out, in a great way—like a puppy that follows you down the road. And, in her case, the one she could not shoo away.

One day I worked up the nerve to say, "Hi." It wasn't that hard—she was fun and exciting.

She lived close by and I'd walk with her to school instead of joining Mathe. He wasn't very happy about that but got over it. He had his eye on another anyway.

When I got my driver's license I asked her out—our first real date! I borrowed my dad's car and we set out for the movies. Even with a flat tire and the embarrassment of sweating through my best shirt from changing the flat, we had a great time.

We grew together through high school and then college. Oh, there were rough patches along the way, but I always thought of her as mine, and I think she felt the same way.

Hell, I had known her since the fourth grade. Our bond seemed to be our ability to laugh and enjoy each other—understand each other's needs—kind of a natural respect that grew over time.

My grades in college did not approximate hers even though I was no slouch. After much quibbling, we decided on a little challenge. We both signed up for a class that bore no relationship to our majors and went for it. We both earned an A, but two decimal points tipped the scales in her favor. I never heard the end of that one from Maddy.

Time flew—as it always does. We stayed together and eventually talked about the future.

I had been thinking about asking her "The Question" for some time, but I kept getting cold feet. It wasn't that I wanted anyone else—I just couldn't imagine my life without her—but this was BIG and who knew what the next months would bring? I was about to start my naval career.

I worked up the gumption to tell my mom and dad what I had in mind, and they were all for it. Her parents, on the other hand, probably had other ideas about their daughter's future. You know, it was the old you can do better routine, than the undisciplined youth down the street—me.

My mom took off her engagement ring, put it in my hand, and gave me a big hug. The rest was up to me.

I spent the day washing and waxing my car—and thinking. What am I going to say? What if she says no? What if? What if? What if?

I had cleared out the glove compartment and tied my mom's ring to a little stuffed gremlin I'd snagged from my sister's room and put it inside. When I closed the glove compartment, I remember thinking, *Well, it's now or never!*

So, on that beautiful summer evening, I picked her up for "just a regular date." She commented on how amazingly clean my car was, reminding me that it was usually a mess. I smiled and laughed, trying to seem normal.

Within a mile, I pulled over beside the small lake in our town. I couldn't wait any longer. I was a total nervous wreck!

"Why are you stopping? Are you OK, Finn? You don't seem like your usual goofy self."

"Would you open the glove compartment for me? I think I forgot my wallet. Maybe it's in there."

As she reached inside, her hand touched the small furry guy with the ring attached. Startled, she brought it out and asked, "What in the world is this?"

She finally caught the ring twinkling in the early evening light and smiled.

"Will you, Maddy?" was all I could say.

She looked from me to the ring for what seemed a long time, and with that crooked smile she said, "Well, geez, Finn, what do I say to all the other guys who have asked me the same question?"

All I could think to say was, "What other guys?"

She started to laugh.

"You are a sweaty, nervous mess, Finn. I'm just trying to get you to relax. Don't you know how I feel about you by now, you big goofball?"

She leaned over, hugged me, and whispered "Yes" in my ear. "I have hoped for this for a long time. I just thought I would have to ask you! I love you, Finn."

1968

Now I had to figure out when we could do this. I had not even been to Pensacola! Nine weeks after starting the program, if all went like it was supposed to, I would receive my commission—and get a small break. So that is what we decided. However, I needed flight hours to qualify for a commission, and because of the weather I had to cancel the wedding date three times.

Maddy's mom developed a nice case of hives and was tipping a few more Martinis than usual while trying to corral over 150 guests—and they were talking.

"Does he really want to get married? How cold are Finn's feet? Weather flight hours in Pensacola—are you sure—don't think so? I don't get it? I've got $50 says he will be a no-show." And they kept speculating.

The wagers kept growing on the probability of me not showing up—got even higher when I failed to arrive at the church for the run-through the night before.

I didn't make it to the wedding rehearsal e the night before so she married my stand in—my best man John. But after one plane ride and two buses, I finally made it to the rehearsal dinner. I was beyond tired, newly minted, and still in my whites.

I walked into the dining room, and while moving past friends and parents I caught my dad's smile. It felt like I had crossed over, and the expectations were well, you know—everything seemed to be strikingly new and very exciting. And then…

There she was—my prize, little Maddy. She was all smiles as I crossed the room to gather her up.

It was close to seismic for both of us. As Maddy fidgeted with my new ensign shoulder boards, I wrapped my arm around her waist and pulled her to me. Someone shoved a drink into my other hand and laughed. I took a deep breath as I tried to get my bearings on this totally nonmilitary environment, the flurry of the previous 24 hours, and the pressure of the last 10 weeks. My head was still in the stars after personally receiving my commission from one of the greats— fighter pilot Colonel "Chappie" James—that same day.

I was starting to settle in when my eyes caught the cold stare from my almost mother-in-law. At this point, her displeasure and happiness to see us together were all over her veiled smile. I was and was not her favorite soon-to-be son-in-law. Too tired to worry, I sank into the long-missed comfort of trust and love for my soon-to-be bride.

My head was still down in Pensacola, but Maddy's arm around my waist and her soft, warm kiss quickly woke me to a reality I had forgotten—a new yet familiar truth. Between conversations and drinks with friends that night, my mind kept flashing back to Pensacola and the hurdles to come.

Trying to pay attention to what my friends were saying, I could only stare and nod while replying with "uh…, ah…, yes, we will when we get back," while my mind wandered back to the work that had to be done to be successful. I kept pushing it back, deeper inside to feel the goodness of the moment and anticipation of our marriage the next day.

I fought off the worry that NAVAIR brings—wanting it and insecure about measuring up at the same time. Time would not stop for me in the gold winged pursuit—even my wedding.

I compartmentalized my feelings as I held Maddy tighter and glanced over at her mother again, even though nothing else mattered. I was finally home—right where I wanted to be.

Maddy whispered something, but it did not register or matter—her touch drowned out her words. Commissioned on a Friday, married on a Saturday, and back to Pensacola flight training on Monday after canceling the wedding three times because of the weather—somehow it all worked

I had rented the only available hovel in Milton, Florida, a place that Lieutenant Hershman had told me about. It was between "Mainside" and Whiting Field—a hedge bet in case my jet selection didn't work out.

I left my shell-shocked new bride by herself on Monday morning to report for duty. I had abandoned her to a lonely time among the few things in our suitcases. No honeymoon for this new Navy couple. She had no car, no TV, no air conditioning, and only one neighbor for miles—who spoke only Hungarian. Even so, she did have one book, a small radio, and a phone with no one to call.

Amid the pressure of getting through the current flight phase, I failed to introduce my new bride to my fellow tribe of student naval aviators and their girlfriends and wives. My classmates didn't think I had a wife—that she was some kind of phantom I'd made up—until one day after class.

"Hey, Finn—you didn't really get married, did you? Where is she?" said Jenny, Tom's wife.

Feeling like I'd "hijacked the pootie," I quickly responded, "Well, why don't we all get together so you can meet her?"

Jenny and Susie scheduled an impromptu party and they brought lilacs and wine. We ate burnt hot dogs and baked beans. Maddy loved it, for she now had some new great friends to help her with the forced isolation she was experiencing. Here we were, three couples from entirely different parts of the country, meeting and completely accepting one another in our new naval aviation roles—husbands and wives not missing a beat from our varied pasts.

This was a new sisterhood for Maddy. Each wife brought similar experiences and new ideas from their homes and college days in Texas, Boston, Los Angeles, and Detroit.

Jenny's husband Tom "Cobber" MacLachlan and Jager, their German shepherd, were wonderful to be with during these challenging months. Unfortunately, Tom lost his life while flying a Navy S3 Viking later in his career—a very somber day for our group.

As we sat there enjoying our newfound friends and much needed southern hospitality, I could not help thinking about another time and another place—a story of my parents' 1944 wartime married life during Dad's flight training in the US:

The similarities of these two different wartime environments, separated by twenty-five years, was astonishing. I thought back to Dad's story.

* * *

Several days later we suited up for a training flight, and instead of 11 crew members, twenty-two boarded our B-17. Each was in full flight leathers with goggles, and we were stuffed into every corner of the aircraft as we climbed out of Walker Field to a much higher altitude.

Giggles were coming from some of the strangest places—a flying love boat—for each crew member had brought his wife or girlfriend.

* * *

I tried to imagine this new batch of student naval aviators and their wives pulling off a similar stunt in the future.

These three girls were instant friends and frequently met at the beach, officers' club, or Traders. It might have been appropriate for the ladies to show up at the base commander's house for introductions with white gloves and calling cards—but nah. Not these girls!

These three would have nothing to do with this tradition. They would cow to no military rules as their husbands struggled for recognized competence and acceptance in each new task and role given to them by the Navy. Limitless conformity was just not their way. After all, it was the '60s and it was hard to give up the freedoms they all had experienced in college. The girls seemed to have it together somehow and looked good, smelled good, and even knew how to talk to us even though I was still a little tongue-tied around them.

I wanted to give Maddy more of my time so we could participate in the intimate and ordinary experiences of newlyweds. But, I was married to her and NAVAIR and hoped she would understand. A honeymoon—what was that?

She was patient and tolerant with me when I balked at normal married life behaviors and actions I had never thought about before. I was in training in more ways than one.

She smiled and bit her lip during excursions to the PX (military base post exchange retail stores). It worried me that we were spending our money to buy all odds and ends to set up our life together. As we walked the aisles and she kept pulling stuff into our cart, I was aghast.

Ironing board, broom, and a T-shirt—how would we be able to afford the cost?

"Maddy, are you kidding me? I don't know how we will be able to afford all this stuff," I whispered, entirely out of my element.

"It will be OK, Finn, you'll see," she said with a smile.

As I look back I guess I was slowly getting it. Marriage—did I really sign up for this?

The Navy isn't very easy on friendships, and each couple was given orders in different directions. Leaving those great people behind was hard and sad, but there was no choice—we promised to stay in touch as they followed their own aviation pipe lines to win our wings—and did for a while—just not long enough.

And then it was on to basic jet training in Meridian, Mississippi. Maddy and I were not prepared for the attitudes we would find in the Deep South in the '60s. It was a racial hotbed for a Midwestern naval officer and his wife.

In the few days we had before reporting for duty at NAS (Naval Air Station) Meridian, we found an open weekend to take a break with a drive to the Gulf Coast for some shrimp and a change of scenery. On the way back, driving on an amazingly dark, kudzu-lined roadway to Meridian through central Mississippi, we came upon a horrible accident scene. Our headlights shined on several people running to and fro across the interstate yelling, screaming, and crying for someone to help. Someone was pinned between and under a guard rail and truck axle. After several tries, we could not move the truck that was slowly crushing the victim. We asked for directions to the next town and sped up the highway to find a police officer.

His first question was: "What color are the folks that were in the accident?" After pleading for help we told him they were black. His reaction floored us.

He said, "I'll get there when I can—got rounds to do."

It was a real eye-opener. The police officer's behavior was not part of our world or anything we had known. Being young and somewhat self-oriented, I didn't think about the ignorance, fear, and violence that was all around us—let alone right in our face. It seemed to be true that entrenched segregation was a fire you could not put out, and we decided it best to keep a low Northerner profile in this strange land. We had read that someone our age had recently paid a terrible price for taking a desegregation stand. These people were playing by strange rules—an incomprehensible set of right and wrongs.

We slunk back to our small apartment in Meridian not knowing what to say. Sometimes things are just too big to talk about. For weeks the weight of that night lay heavy upon both of us. Later that summer it took the live TV broadcast of a fellow naval aviator, Neil Armstrong, and his walk on the moon to recalibrate our minds to the real goodness of our country. And he had traveled the same NAVAIR pipeline I was in—pretty exciting times. We smiled more after that night while watching the country's first steps on the moon. And our faith was restored in the good old USA—even with its problems. A little perspective sure helped.

Meridian taught me a new way to walk. I was gone for eight to ten hours a day, coming home exhausted and spent with another four hours of book time. It must have been painful for my new bride to share me with my other girlfriend—Naval Aviation. It never dawned on me that she would become unhappy—for we just kept soldiering on together for as long as it took. Oh sure we had our spats, and she complained that the Navy was becoming a lot more than a job. As we lay in bed at night, she quizzed me on my new jet's emergency procedures that I had written on three-by-five cards. The cards often ended in the word "eject." I remember her saying, "Finn, a lot of these end in 'eject.' Is that likely to happen? I know you know what you're doing but this is really scary."

It was finally hitting home that things could happen.

I smiled back and said her words to her. "It will be OK, Maddy. You'll see."

We were secure in each other and still found time to laugh. But a series of crashes, some fatal, on and off base, had Maddy at wit's end. She would hear about the accidents on the radio. And of course, I had my head down, diligently studying or flying, and would not hear of the incidents until sometime after the occurrence—and therefore never gave her a call to tell her I was safe.

I seldom had had any time away from the training regimen. But a short leave opportunity allowed us to return home for a few days. Arriving at Metropolitan Airport in Detroit, dressed in my whites, the uninviting stares we received caused me to pause. I was unprepared for the quiet hostility we received as a newly minted naval officer with his new bride. What were these people thinking? Less than accepting, their attitudes reflected just the opposite of our feelings at the time. I guess the anti-military sentiment of the times was for real—and my need to protect Maddy suddenly jumped forward with each less-than-welcoming facial expressions we received.

Oh, I almost forgot "Taco"—our Mexican heritage bachelor connection from Austin, Texas. Al Chavez was as solid as you would want in a pilot, a human being and a cook—loaded with character. He was a frequent visitor along with other stray pilots. They all drove great cars—fast and loud. So we knew they were coming before we heard the knock on the door. Taco always brought the supplies for his specialty—tacos. We'd eat, laugh, tease each other, and throw back a few beers. Good times and the best tacos I've ever had—then and now.

"Taco" eventually became Al's handle. His career grew, and he was selected to fly with the "Blues" after several Vietnam tours as an F-4, and A-4 driver. Our paths crossed several times, and his Mexican food specialty continues to get served to the Naval Aviation Community.

Thirteen: Hover Boy to Pointy End Driver

Arrogant Snarls
"Don't Worry Baby" – Beach Boys

After MSU graduation, the Navy took Mathe and me in two different directions. Mathe was commissioned in the Marine Corp and was immediately pumped into the helo pipeline, bound for Vietnam, while I had some training hoops to jump through before my aircraft selection time came.

I eventually became a neighborhood terrorizer as an A-4 driver, part of the pointy-end attack community—and my new neighborhood was wherever "Uncle" sent us. It took time to develop the confidence and skill to fly and fight with the scooter. I relished pointing the nose to the ground to blow things up in the thick hot heat of Texas, California, and Nevada. But were we really ready for the real thing in Vietnam? And that is exactly where I was headed after some pretty thorough preparation.

I received orders to report to the USS Raleigh CVA-23 (Hawk) and had three days to get there—by boat, train or any other conveyance. I was excited to put all my training to the test.

I had to kiss my little gal Maddy goodbye and promise her I'd return home in one piece. Hmmm—this was getting very real.

Raleigh CVA-23 (Hawk) – Vietnam

In time, I became accepted in "Talon's"— Attack Squadron VA-33. As I stepped into the Talon's ready room one early morning I could not believe my eyes. Mathe, God—could it be? Incredible! My buddy, a Marine CH-46 driver was standing right before my eyes. No mistaking that square jaw, dark eyes, and clef stamped in his chin— right here in the flesh. I couldn't believe it.

"Finn, heard you were onboard—thought I'd stop by and say hello," he said, as he extended his hand.

"Good to see you! Welcome to the Talons, pal. Let's grab a cup," I said.

"I smacked his arm, grabbed a couple of mugs of coffee, and we retired to a corner of the ready room. We'd made sure to stay in touch but that wasn't very often. We'd both been a little busy!

"What are you doing here, Mathe?" I hadn't contacted him in a year or so after I was assigned temporary unpleasant duty as a spotter—in country with a Marine platoon.

"Just transferred in from the RAG (Replacement Air Group)," he said.

"You what? From where?" I shot back in disbelief. I could not believe it.

What was a Marine CH-46 helo driver assigned to a Navy attack squadron doing on board?

"Ya, Finn, I got really tired of hauling our wounded and dead out of hot LZs (landing zones) and got myself transferred to a Navy attack squadron. Continuously getting opened up like a sardine can as I sat in hover over hot landing zones was making me nuts. Cockpit bullet-hole air conditioning was getting old, and I thought just maybe there was a better way to fight this war. Voila—here I am," he said.

"Some stories, huh?"

"Let's grab another cup of coffee and take a walk."

"Yeah, sure. It's good to see you, man…"

I turned to speak again, but before I knew it, he had filled our mugs, was out the hatch, and had strolled across the upper-level ramp to the hangar deck stairs. We ended up on the hangar deck in front of a mashup of A-4s. He suddenly stopped walking, leaned against the bulkhead, and started to release his burden.

"Well, the long and short of it was—I was trying to save some of my Marines. They were getting shot up pretty bad, so I dropped into a hot landing zone with a tight tree line that tore up some rotor tips on my machine. We got out OK, but this did not go over well with the CO, Lieutenant Colonel Jack McVey. It was the first time I gave him some lip—I guess I'd had enough of his shit. It's not easy doing what's right when it is perceived as wrong."

My mind immediately shot back to my dad's poem about his CO in WWII:

* * *

Fifty times we've sweated weather and Jap flacks' hellish roar.

We've asked about rotation as we've often done before
He says I'll see you get it after fifty more,
The man behind the armor-plated desk.

He says the war is rough, boys, and we all must understand
That he'll see us through it all and keep us well in hand,
Lying on the sofa with his headset in command,
The man behind the armor-plated desk.

D. Stuart White

* * *

Mathe was now in full vent, and there was no stopping him. For a man of few words, he apparently needed to talk. I tried to slow him down.

"Hey, I just spied the A-4M with Marine Corps markings on the deck. Is that yours?"

"Yes, apparently the Navy has been slow in accepting air-to-air radar as you probably know— No radar on your B (A-4 model designation) birds?"

"Yeah, that's right, no radar in our Bs."

"I was ordered to fly the "Mike" out to join the Talons. It looks like our strikes will now have a real capability to ID soviet made MiGs. That's if you can keep up with her," he smirked.

And then he really opened up.

"Finn, I had sized McVey up as way beyond uptight, a rank-climbing careerist who flew by the book with few aeronautical instincts. This was the type that would not hang his ass out for his men, and I didn't like him. In fact, I wanted to grab him by the neck, and— well, you get it."

Mathe continued, "After that mission, things reached a boiling point—and he called me in and let loose. Holding onto his rank, our eyes met. The meanness and vitriol in McVey's meager stature stood out, and it was more than I could take. I'd had enough and told McVey:"

'What did you expect me to do, let those Marines die?
Take a look at that chopper. See those bullet holes?'
That's our job, you turd. Sir, skip the bilge, I thought to myself.

94

'I made the decision to go in to save some people, and you chew me out for breaking up expensive taxpayer rotor blades? Give me a break! You make no sense.

"On second thought, OK, you win. I won't risk my crew's necks again to save some Marines from getting shot up!'

"I knew that would piss him off, Finn, but I didn't care."

McVey had more to say, 'You keep that up, Lieutenant, and you won't have a future here,' His face was beet red.

To make things worse, I looked at him and said, 'OK, go for it, sir, but I'll decide what is right for my crew and what isn't and you can take that to the bank.'

"I held my tongue after that and looked at the floor," and thought, *I'll fly for you, dunker head, but I will not die for you.*

He said, 'Dismissed, Lieutenant Stone!'

"McVey gave me another caustic look as I saluted and stomped out of the tent-flapped door ready room into the mushy Marble Mountain mud and rain. I thought to myself, *Well, that about does it for my career. Only time will tell how—I'm a goner.*

My naive instinct was to teach the captain a hard lesson in priorities, but that didn't go so well. I got what I wanted, though—my payload—my shot-up living and dead Marines home—and that was all that really mattered. I just couldn't put up with him anymore, Finn—he really got to me."

Mathe's face told me the whole story.

"Look, Finn, I made a mistake. I couldn't compromise. I wanted to make a difference—and I did what I thought was right and got my ass burned for it. I guess that pretty well sums it up."

I shook my head. "God, man, you could be in the brig. You have to let go of this, Mathe, or you'll be a danger to yourself and everyone else you fly with. You chose to make those soldiers matter, and that is what counts.

Mathe, you seem to have found your own meaning for this war and, believe it or not, you are ahead of the game for most who do what we do."

It got real quiet as my words struck home. Mathe's story mirrored my feelings about compromise—pretty close. While serving and flying off the Raleigh on my first cruise, I suspected there would come a day when my self-preservation and the idiocy of some of our missions in this upside-down war would outweigh the desires of the command structure. Just like Mathe, it would probably come out in a face-to-face with one of my senior officers.

I thought to myself, maybe a Navy squadron fleet seat for this experienced Marine aviator would be the cure—may be less rigid than he had experienced with his Marine Corps squadron. It would certainly give him the latitude to dish it out to the enemy for once—a new start. How had he escaped what could have been really bad? There was a reason he was selected to join us—someone liked him—somewhere.

I wanted him to fit in and would make every effort to clear the way for his acceptance among the JOs (junior officers) and his superiors.

"That's OK. Welcome to the Navy Mathe! We need good aviators and especially a Jarhead who has tasted the war close-up. I've been told Talons are a high-stress, achiever environment with slightly more tolerance to getting along with other squadron members—nothing new for you, I expect. Even though our guys are a bit happy-go-lucky, they are warriors and sometimes very independent—ego-driven. Ya know, I think I'm talking to the choir—am I right?"

"Kind of, Finn," he said.

He was holding something back and I knew it as he looked back at me with a glance rather than straight on.

"So you're still a captain in the Corps with orders to fly A-4s? You must have done something right to get assigned to fly for the Talons—a Navy attack squadron? Maybe you've got the pictures of someone," I speculated.

He smiled and looked away. Boy, was it great to have him on board.

"Anyway, you're welcome here. Tell me about the transition from hover boy to the pointy-end community. I bet it was quite a change. We have a lot of catching up to do," I said. "And you brought an A-4M with RWR gear on board. Hope the Raleigh keeps her—even though she carries the Marine labeled hump and all. It sure will help with our lack of airborne radar capability. Someone might just live a little longer."

Math found his path in the squadron and his smoothness in the air in short order. Even though he missed flying an open-cockpit aircraft with a more direct touch of the air over its control surfaces as opposed to the more constrained controls of jets, he became accepted as a good stick for the Talons. He never took himself too seriously, and that was why he was liked—kind of unique for a Marine—and for Mathe.

Our squadron, the Talons, wore their wings with strength—earned and not given—and our token Marine fit right in. In time Matthew "Rock" Stone turned into a "Talons Gangster" like the rest of us—an inside JO (junior officer) moniker we used when testosterone was running high. Wasn't that what the gomers were calling us— "Pirates/Gangsters"? So why not?

Our assignments grew over time as we were promoted. Seeing another one of our squadron mates perish in a fiery crash on deck steeled my resolve to survive.

Tom "Cobber" MacLachlan had been with us since flight school, and I remember him distinctly telling everyone he would be the first to go Mach 1. This Texan's death hardened me and turned up the flame of my "the-hell-with-it-all" attitude toward our combat roles—to make each count. With each day's gut check I would turn into that real gangster the gomers were already calling us.

Navy rituals and procedures were getting less critical as the fight to survive took front and center over Vietnam.

While flying one frustrating mission after another, I started to develop the feeling that our rules were now covering someone else—not those on the line. Politicians or the brass—it did not matter, for anyone could easily become the "bad actor," when engaging the enemy. Our verbal and nonverbal mantra, "Who gives a shit!" showed how compromised our orders were. I had to kill and let the chips fall as a hired warrior. It was necessary to stretch the limits, hold the violent edge, and do my job. If I become that 'bad actor' who gets pinned with the wrap—so be it.

I found myself frequently asking the question *Why?* as I struggled to find a reason for the flying we undertook—with no answer coming to me most of the time.

Our serious business refocused our attention on looking out for each other in the face of the enemy—on board, in the air, and over the jungles. Even though our morale was slowly being gutted. The flying challenges continued to present themselves, and we were trained—no, steeled—to the challenge and competition regardless of the means to an end.

* * *

Mathe seemed to be having problems coming aboard—landings. Right after one of those post-flight briefs, I pigeonholed him to find out why he was struggling to come aboard consistently. His landing grades were suffering—something wasn't right. I needed to help him find the answer—to put an end to his time in the barrel.

"Hey, Mathe, what's the skinny with your landings?" I said.

"What do you mean, Finn?" he said with bowed head.

"I know you, Mathe. Something is not right."

I kind of thought his family situation was somehow in the mix, holding him back—negatively impacting his flying.

"Well, I can't get my dad, whoever he was, off my mind," he said.

"Is that all?" I said, trying to break the tension.

Mathe seemed to be confused and distracted. His confidence was flagging, and if he didn't improve, his career would be jeopardized. The Navy had little tolerance for pilots or much of anything for that matter that was out of spec. They wouldn't wait long to make the correction.

"You wanna talk about it?"

"Finn, it's not your problem," he hissed.

I jumped on him, aggressively. "Yes, it is my problem. We do this thing as a team, remember? You have to fight for the right to get shot at in this squadron, and getting aboard safely is part of the fight. Now, what's really bothering you? You haven't been able to concentrate, and we both know that our slates have to be clean—no worries or concerns in our lives, or our flying careers will be in jeopardy."

Again, I got that look from him, but no words. *Why was he holding back? What was it?* I wondered. He kept a strong grip on some fearful little edge.

"Look Mathe, Fat Jack tells me your looking good on the approaches right up until…" and I paused to draw him out.

"You're talking about my airmanship with Fat? You're kidding. That's my business! It's not your problem, Finn," he snarled.

"Your problem is the squadron's problem, Mathe. When one part does not perform, it puts everyone you fly with in jeopardy." I could see him thinking, mulling over how much to say.

"Ok you asked for it! My mom is worse than ever. She writes letters that continue to make no sense—scattered, weird stuff that is getting crazier. She's had three car accidents in the last three months. The most recent one—she drove into the side of the house 'by mistake' because she said she 'forgot her glasses.' So far she hasn't hurt anyone else, but that is next—I can smell it. She is a total mess. I need to get her some help—get her in rehab or something. Then there is Rusty. Her letters aren't the same—short, quick notes with no feeling in them. Like she's lost interest or has someone else. And I thought she was The One! AND, here I sit rocketing rice paddies, in a war that makes no sense anymore—and the rest of my life is going to shit!"

Finn's jaw drops. *Rusty, Jesus, I didn't even know that Rusty was writing him—let alone that she meant so much to him. Why doesn't this guy ever open up? He could really use some time off!*

I looked Mathe in the eye and said, "So now that you've got that off your chest—you feel better?"

"Yeah, as a matter of fact, I do."

A smirk crept into the corners of his mouth.

Ok then—"Right now, the important thing is to get you up to speed coming aboard—lets figure that out first. Then we'll work on the rest. I got your six, man. Don't you know that by now?

Fourteen: "Fast in the Groove" (FIG)

"Long Cool Woman" – The Hollies

1970

As Mathe and I bored through the early pre-dawn sky, wisps of cloud lit by the moon whisked by our cockpits. I rechecked my heading once again for the run into the suspected communist hideout, deep in the jungles of North Vietnam. They called it an armed reconnaissance mission—but we knew it as a time to hunt, to scout, or whatever you wanted to name it. No EA-6 Prowler was jamming the opposition or heavy F-4 CAP (Combat Air Patrol) coverage tonight—just the distant security of our airborne controller and possibly a FAC (forward air controller) up early, out there, scouting up targets in the weeds or waiting for *that call for help.* No FAC broadcasts yet, but we knew they were out there.

Switching frequencies, I picked up the distant calls of "Ducksford," an Air Force C-130 orbiting north off the coast, bleeding through our channel frequency, with call-outs for their Air Force attack and fighter strikes to the north.

Sporadic broken clouds skidded by and then released us into clear calm air and hazy moonlight. Springing from stable to unstable air, we

101

picked our way through thunderstorms via moon luminescence as we penetrated occasional cells.

Mathe's approaches had improved and his attitude was not quite as surly, but —things were still not right. He just wasn't fully engaged.

Suddenly Mathe called out, "Finn, go squadron discrete—button 20."

I clicked my mic button twice to acknowledge.

"What a ride tonight partner," Mathe suddenly called.

"You betcha, Mathe. Except for Taco and Butts getting lost," I interjected.

Yeah, those guys just disappeared into the darkness—guess we'll join up sooner or later, I thought.

"You know this ride beats the state fair back home," Mathe blurted out.

"Got a radio, earphones, air conditioning, lots of Noir leather in this cockpit, pal, raging testosterone, and a 360-degree view of everything on the street plus this sporty ride—feeling good."

"Let's knock it off and talk about it when we get back, Mathe," Finn answered.

I quickly glanced over the canopy rail at Mathe's jet, and even though I couldn't see his face, I knew he had a smile going on inside his O2 mask. Nice to hear him in the right mood. We motored on into the night and I concentrated on getting my head back into the mission—on headings, airspeeds, time on target, and frequency changes prior to arm up. I eyeballed the reflected lightning strikes against a line of raging black cells in front of us and prepared the jet and myself for the weather penetration.

* * *

Mathe was glued to my wing and probably had caught the increased light radiating from my cockpit. It alerted him to cover the penetration checklist. Mathe quickly confirmed the anti-ice was ON and waited in anticipation for my call to reduce power to achieve the required 250-knot penetration airspeed. Mathe (Claw 3) then turned the cockpit light to match mine and tightened his torso and shoulder harness while lowering the seat.

"Claw 3, looks like weather ahead. Let's hold 250 knots, on a heading 280," I commanded.

"Roger, Claw 3."

"Where the hell are Taco (Claw 2) and Butts (Claw 4)?" I thought.

Commander Al "Taco" Chavez was a seasoned aviator, proud, confident and professional. He was trusted to make the right decisions. We constantly pranked him about his heritage and he took it in stride and out flew many in the Talons. Ensign James "Butts" Butler, on the other hand, had just arrived and his status was yet to be determined as our newbie. He was popular among the junior officers which was important to his integration in the squadron. But, our nugget (first tour aviator) was untested and only time would tell.

Today, we were told in our pre-strike brief—that if the formation broke up for whatever reason we should continue individually or in section to the target.

And I had lost Taco and Butts in a cloud layer after the launch and was concerned.

Mathe opened the spread on my wing as I continued scanning the sky leveling off at "Angels" fifteen (15,000 feet) and finally found them. They were still a section of two, at least one mile away hustling along on a parallel heading—1,000 feet below us.

I switched channels back to squadron discrete.

"You boys lost?" I asked.

I thought I could see their heads swiveling aggressively—scanning the sky even faster upon hearing my voice.

"We're eight o'clock, one mile," I called again.

Taco caught sight of my section, clicked his mic button twice in embarrassed acknowledgment, and immediately steepened and tightened his turn to merge with Mathe and me, with Butts temporarily glued to his wing. Butts followed one-half mile behind and was closing after losing it in the climb. I glared at Butts' aircraft while silently cursing his airmanship. Taco finally joined on Mathe's wing with our straggler in tow. The bumpy air chop was not helping Claw flight's "new guy."

I led in loose echelon on up to FL180 (18,000 feet)—deeper into North Vietnam—as Butts, several plane lengths behind, continued to struggle to stay in formation.

I knew that Butts would most likely be first up, reporting a lower fuel state than the rest of the flight if and when we needed a tanking evolution for recovery—returning to the boat.

"Come on, Butts, tighten it up—get your ass in position—we have work to do!" I called as I jockeyed attitude and power to give Butts a chance to close the distance for the join—and it worked for the nugget.

I continued my climb through FL190 while keeping my turn coming for a rollout on a 290-degree heading.

"Let's find that target and lose the Mk 82s (unguided low-drag general-purpose bomb), fellas."

The radio suddenly exploded to life from Claw flight's FAC (forward air controller)—a TA-4. "Playboy"—gave new vectors to our target and clearance to descend to Angels sixteen (16,000 feet).

While arming up and waiting for the final heading change to the target I recognized Playboy and knew they were from the H&MS-13 squadron based out of Chu Lai. They usually worked just north of the DMZ and into Laos—for it was just too hot for a FAC to loiter further north.

The rising sun blazed over our formation as the last shred of morning cloud and precipitation broke from our flight path. The early morning sunlight was welcome, for it increased our chances of putting a real hurt on the gomers. At the same time, it also raised the opportunity for them to more efficiently target Claw flight—a trade-off each pilot had accepted and agreed to early in their careers. Under FAC control, we continued our descent to Angels sixteen. After picking up vectors to the target, I concentrated on finding the target for the lineup, with Mathe right next to me and Taco and Butts following in echelon.

No attack circle today. This strike would be an echelon roll-in—in sequence—with timed separation, one right after another; no observation loitering call-outs above. I found the target and told Claw flight to ease the spread out for the roll-in.

The roll-in would be at Angels fifteen, start the hard pull up at twelve, release at eleven without busting the 9,000-foot base altitude—trimmed for 450 knots. I reconfirmed the 70-mill ring setting for target lead in the sight and noted the quarter ball deviation needed to hold the lineup.

Each of us had heard of the new Grail/Strela (light weight, shoulder-fired surface-to-air) missiles that the commies were using. They had the capability of reaching us, so the base altitude would give us some protection against any enemy targeting our jets.

I rolled in from the sun for the lineup to the target with the A-4's belly pointing to the sky while looking out the side of the canopy and pulling hard. Suddenly, out of the corner of my eye I caught our nugget aviator hurtling through the strike group. *So much for our flight integrity today.* Butts was utterly lost in his orientation to the target and the rest of Claw flight. He was close to splitting us up as he overtook Taco and Mathe. Finn feared Butts might ram their jets as they altered their respective bearings to the target to evade a collision.

"Butts, get your shit together, goddammit. You got a problem, pull off!" I yelled.

Butts found his spacing and the rest of the flight quickly formed separation and rolled in with everyone hanging in their straps and working their asses off.

My flurry of effort included initially kicking rudder for minor corrections to compensate for slight aircraft drift in the lineup. I kept my concentration, eyeballing the bursts of flak and continued target acquisition for a proper release. I flinched at the close burst of flak that seemed to be just above my canopy and, of course, employed all the stick and rudder skills required to hit the target and not hit Butts. Even so, with the sudden change of altitude, flak bursts, and the altimeter unwinding, I found myself unconsciously trying to get as small as possible to keep safe—shrinking in my seat.

It was a good feeling to turn and see Claw flight strung out behind as I pickled the bombs, felt the aircraft jump, and pulled off target at around 8,200 feet, doing a little more than 500 knots.

My G-suit squeezed to keep blood in my upper body so as not to pass out while continuing the jink to evade the enemy targeting us.

Butts continued to struggle for position as tail-end Charley.

Claw flight reassembled after the bomb run—with Butts in tow—and turned toward the carrier.

"Time to get home," I mumbled. I had been cleared for a flight of four for the approach—to come aboard the Raleigh.

On the way back to the Raleigh, Mathe's approach problems were on my mind. But, we had other problems to consider—there were rumors of enlisted sabotage circulating throughout the ship. Mathe must have known but, never spoke of it.

Enlisted sabotage? That can't happen on the Raleigh. This was a simple fuel metering problem—a true technical issue with no malice or intent, I thought.

Thoughts about the recent spate of flameouts the Talons were experiencing on their landing approaches disappeared as Finn brought Claw flight into the break, hot. The four fanned away from the boat with Butts struggling to hold his position on downwind. We each found the boat and landed in very different ways with varying grades—highly visible proof of our airmanship—good or bad.

After dismounting the Skyhawk, I caught up with Butts walking across the deck. I looked at his hangdog expression and knew he was well aware of the problems he had created during the strike. I went easy on him—he's new after all. No need to destroy our young nugget coming right out of the chute. Butts would have his come-to-Jesus moment even though Fat Jack gave him an OK 3 (above average) landing grade. Even so, my real concern was Mathe.

Fat Jack (our air wing LSO) words were still the same: "Fast in the groove. Too much power out of the turn—high in the middle—fast, nose down in close."

Knowing Mathe, he probably heard those words twenty-four seven. His greenie board landing grades were posted for everyone to see.

The best landing grades competition between the two of us was fierce. I prided myself on smooth, predictable, and controlled flying and was leading the battle to be the best coming aboard. "Sleek as a shark's fin slicing the water"—I overhead someone comment. All aviators motivation for excellence was the same—to fly an approach that was stable in pitch, roll, and on airspeed.

Meatball, lineup, and angle of attack were slowly disappearing as Mathe's key drivers—well established before joining the fleet. Mathe was struggling mightily and there was a good chance they would ground him or worse.

Mathe held it together in his approaches, on airspeed, and altitude at the 90, but at this point, the balance of his approaches were falling apart. Many times Fat Jack found him looking at the deck. Deck spotting was a huge no-no, and it had found its way into his approaches. Mathe knew that dropping his nose usually led to landing short and a No. 1 wire catch or even worse hitting the round down—the end of the ship.

Raleigh's arresting gear was comprised of four (numbered from 1, furthest aft) cables. Between bolters (failure to catch an arresting cable) Mathe was consistently catching everything but the Target 3 wire coming on board the Raleigh.

Fat Jack had provided counsel, but it was up to Mathe to remedy. Jack thought he was becoming a "frightened aviator." There weren't any heated differences yet between Mathe and Fat Jack, but I knew Mathe's irritation was boiling and it was just a matter of time before it got personal. I also knew Jack would win in the end.

After a few more words with Butts, I placed Mathe squarely in my sights—to help him find a solution if I could.

"Good mission today," I called as I brushed Mathe's shoulder in the passageway to the ready room trying to draw him out. I had to talk to him about his landing grades even though I knew it he wouldn't like it one bit, but, I felt our friendship could cut it.

"Yep, but getting aboard is getting interesting," Mathe replied.

Mathe had to pull the trigger on his request for leave. His mom had finally done what he feared.

Fifteen: Finding Home

Green Eyes
"Do You Believe in Magic" – Lovin' Spoonful

Math returned home after his mom's final car accident—to say goodbye and to bury her. He welcomed the break from the high operational tempo, but not for this. Coming home to a cold dark house brought back so many sad memories—it just plain hurt. He found some old boxes at the back of his mom's closet—searching for the last dress she would ever wear.

As he sat on the living room floor sorting through the history of his family—things he had never seen. Looking around him, he pondered what to do with her house. He guessed it was his now. The pictures in front of him, the ones she had never shared, told him much about his father. He felt terrible for both of them and for himself. They could not hold their love together or live long enough to help him grow up.

Mathe's mother had purposely held much of his father's military career close to her and chose not to share it with her son.

He got up for a break and walked into the kitchen. Opening the refrigerator he grabbed a beer and noticed that nothing had changed. It saddened him to recall that there was always a beer but not much else in their fridge—two eggs, one sad-looking tomato, a small wedge of cheese, and a leftover, half-eaten dinner. A reflection of the tragic, lonely life she lived. Returning to the living room, he stopped to build a fire. It was freezing outside—a far cry from the heat and humidity of 'Nam.

Sitting back down in front of the fire he spread out more letters, photos, and albums. Their images were terrific—two happy people—holding hands, laughing, always laughing. *I look just like Dad, and Mom is beautiful.*

All of this is so unreal, he thought, as the fire crackled in his moment of quiet. *Two days ago I was in a war zone, and now this.* The doorbell suddenly rang and broke Mathe free from his thoughts.

"I guess I have to answer that," Mathe mumbled.

Opening the front door, he smiled as he realized that this is what he had been missing—for months.

"Rusty. Geez, come on in, It's freezing out there."

"I didn't think anyone was here. I couldn't see any lights in the house. But I knew you had to be here. The service is tomorrow, right? I'm so sorry, Mathe! God, you look so tired." She sighed, leaned over and gave Mathe a hug.

"Well, I've been on three planes for I don't know how many hours—not much sleep. Want a beer? Can you stay?"

"Yes, that would be great. I don't have to go back to work for two whole days," she said.

Rusty was a nurse or almost a nurse. A few more classes to go and she'd have her certificate.

Mathe took her coat and caught her scent—wow, she smelled so good and looked even better. *I have been away too long,* he thought. Her auburn hair was piled up, exposing the nape of her neck—soft and vulnerable. His eyes caught the break in her blouse, exposing more than she intended. He could feel his face turning red—his breathing getting shorter and more anxious—from the embarrassing strength of his feelings. He tried to refocus. She smiled as she caught his eyes. *Oh man, those eyes—keep your shit together, Mathe! Go slow!*

"Are you hungry? There's isn't much in the fridge," he blurted out while trying to get a hold of himself.

"I'm starved! Bet we can figure something out. There must be an egg—may be a bit of cheese?"

"Yeah, but not much more than that."

They made their way to the kitchen and Rusty opened a few cupboard doors and the freezer. He watched her while she moved around the space—her shape, her smile, her laughter. She seemed very comfortable in this strange kitchen and chatted away about work, friends, and his mom. Within what seemed record time, he had a cheese and tomato omelet and toast in his hand. Too good to be true!

"Don't tell me you can cook too!"

"Mathe, this is hardly cooking. You could have done this."

"I'm very impressed!"

"Well, thanks. My mom taught me a few things but, you know, Mathe, if you can read you can cook. You can read, right? Isn't that a requirement for flying a plane?"

She gives him a long look—sort of sizing him up. Mathe was not good at this small-talk stuff. But, he realized he could be there in that room with her forever. He just didn't know how to say it. So all he could come up with was: "So, how are you?" Typical!

"Good. Busy. Work is nuts. I really enjoy it. My patients all need help, and I try to be there for them. I'm so overwhelmed. I haven't had a lot of time to write—sorry. But you know, I haven't had one from you in a long time."

"Yeah, I'm sorry about that—a lot going on for me too."

Mathe had changed from the vulnerable, uncertain kid she had known from her youth into a man of real strength and conviction. She saw the change in him from his letters and now, with him right in front of her—the real thing. Even with the circles under his eyes, he still looked so good.

"Can I help with anything—for tomorrow or with the house? I'm sure you don't have much time before you have to go back."

"Well, I've been thinking about that. The service is tomorrow at two at the church. I don't think many people will come. Maybe a few from her work—a neighbor or two. Her brother might show up. She didn't have a lot of friends—a quiet, sad lady who never got over losing her man. God, I wish I could have helped her! I spent too much time being angry with her. She wouldn't talk about my dad—lost herself in a bottle. They said it was an accident— that her car slid off the road and rammed a tree. I'm not so sure about that," he answered.

"Oh, Mathe, what could you have done? I don't think she wanted help. She was half a person for a long time." She sighed again.

"Rusty, you should see the stuff I found—pictures from when they were young that I have never seen. It's all on the floor in the living room. Come take a look."

"Are you sure, Mathe? It's kind of private," she said.

"Who better to share it with? We've known each other for a long time."

"My mom never was the same without my dad. I was pretty little when I finally figured out why she was so sad so much of the time. She just missed him." As I walked back to the living room I put my arm around her shoulders and her hand slipped around my waist.

"The farm we lived on in Pennsylvania had been in my mom's family for a long time—rolling green hills with black dirt that could grow anything. We had cows that I milked and chickens that I took care of and acres of cornfields—even an apple orchard. I spent a lot of time there picking, boxing, and loading. My dad wasn't there to do the work. Mom said Dad loved it there and worked hard to make it good."

We sat down in front of the fire and I handed her some of the pictures. In them you could see all the trees, acres of farmland, the open sky—the beauty of the place.

"It didn't take too long before we just couldn't stay any longer. No one in Mom's family wanted it, so we had to sell the farm. Grandma and Grandpa lived near Detroit to be near Grandma's family, and said we should come to live near them. They missed him too. He was their only son."

As he sorted through various documents, two ribboned medals suddenly dropped to the floor. He was awestruck—as their significance told all. *Are you kidding me,* he thought. He read the description of the honors that were clutched tightly in his hands and heaved a sigh. Rusty felt his distress and moved closer to his side.

Tears began to well as he grappled with the dimension of this find. His body bowed, and he shook his head in sadness. Rusty saw the medals in his hand and his sad face. She moved closer to get a better look. She searched his eyes—looking for a way to calm his pain.

"Why? How could she have not told me about this?" he said as the enormity of the find started to weigh on him. The medals glowed in the firelight—felt warm in his hands. A Silver Star and a Distinguished Flying Cross—his dad's contribution to WWII.

"Two of the highest honors a fighting man can receive, and she never told me. Why?" he groaned. "I guess she couldn't handle me wanting to be just like him."

"I couldn't make Mom happy, Rusty. No matter what I did. I couldn't do anything for her."

Unexpected tears rolled down his cheeks.

Rusty put a consoling arm around Mathe. Sometimes there are no words.

Mathe didn't have much in this world he could put his faith in except his buddy Finn, but Rusty was rapidly filling the void.

Her hair glowed in the firelight. He felt the comfort of her presence and thought, *No planes to fly, no missiles or bullets to dodge today.*

Their hands touched as they shared letters and pictures. His pain was slowly draining away—just being here with her.

She looked at one incredible picture of his mom and then at him. "Oh, Mathe—your mom was happy once. You have to try and remember her that way and let all the other awful stuff go. I know she loved you."

It came out of him as naturally as being in a plane.

"What about you, Rusty? Do you?" he asked as he peered up into her eyes. "I'm not the easiest guy to love—moody, ornery, a pain in the ass."

"I know that."

Heaving a great sigh, she leaned closer and whispered, "You forget how long I have known you—all the great times we've had together. I know who you are and I wouldn't have it any other way. I have loved you since I was 16 years old."

He leaned in. *God, those green eyes. I could live in those eyes forever. They feel like home to me.* He gave her a hungry kiss, trying to take it slowly, trying to make it last.

"When I asked if you could stay, Rusty, I didn't mean for an hour."

"I had hoped that's what you meant, Mathe."

Mathe got up and spread what was left of the fire—giving her a chance to change her mind. She was in the same spot when he returned—smiling at him.

"Do you need to call anyone to let them know where you are?"

"No, Mathe, they'll figure that out."

Mathe reached for her hand and together they turned out the lights on the way up the stairs. He could see the full moon through the window at the end of the hall—no more snow, just stars in a cold, black sky.

He closed the door to his mom's room, wishing her peace and a goodnight. Stepping into his room he was glad to see that all was neat and tidy. His mom may have had her problems, but she liked a ship-shape home. Rusty was right next to him and Mathe closed the door behind them.

She stepped to the window and looked out—then back at Mathe. With a shy smile, she turned and started to unbutton her blouse.

"Let me do that," Mathe said.

He stepped toward her. Her hands went to her sides, and she just waited—staring at him. One soft piece of fabric after another landed on the floor. Eventually, there wasn't anything else to take off—she was so beautiful glowing in the moonlight.

She took his hand and said softly, "Your turn, flyboy." With our faces an inch apart, slowly, very slowly she did the same to me.

When I can't stop obsessing about some stupid flying thing or whatever has my dander up, I bring that night into focus and I am instantly calm. It was the very best night of my life.

Sixteen: Tall Air

An Unlikely Gun Fighter
"Street Fighting Man" – Rolling Stones

1971

Finn watched as "Skipper" Kilkenny eyeballed the 30 pilots waiting for his pre-launch ready room words but several of his junior officers quickly caught his attention in the last row. Kilkenny gave the eye to his bubble blower JO jokesters in the back of the room and knew they needed a little bracing. They called themselves, the "Cocks On Top." Kilkenny knew them as anything but on top—but they were cocks.

"Skipper" Kilkenny, our red headed Irish fireball leader was no more than 5' 7" tall and ran the carrier air group with a loud opinionated drum beat. He was not one to cross unless you handed him a cigar and a glass of whiskey. When he wasn't commanding, he was fishing; when he wasn't fishing he was sailing; and when he wasn't doing any of the preceding he was in a bar slamming down whiskey and pulling on the biggest cheroot known to any naval aviator. But, he was known to be fair in all his dealings with enlisted and officers alike. The Navy had been his wife and children.

He had one weak spot—he liked cats. The story goes that he named them Jack and Dingle. Sailors often mentioned that they heard meows coming from the Skipper's quarters although no one had ever seen them. Kilkenny began his brief.

"Gentlemen, I'm telling you this once—here is the deal! And for you in the cheap seats—this applies to you!" With a severe look, Kilkenny commanded, "Black shirts under green flight suits, no yellows, OK? Knit'em or shit'em but git'em." The Skipper's message was loud and clear as I grabbed my flight suit's zipper and pulled it a little higher to cover my glaring red T-shirt.

I looked over to the next seat and caught "Knuckles" Heming,[1] our toe-handed Talon squadron mate, rubbing his thumb as usual—trying to control the urge not to pee himself as thoughts of going out and killing someone gained traction. Yes, a hunting accident had caused the loss of his thumb, and in order to keep flying for the Navy he took the extreme measure of grafting his big toe to his thumb—when the partially destroyed thumb would not heal in place. The thumb rubbing was probably his pre-launch ritual or to counteract some lingering athlete's foot fungus.

"And just one more piece of advice, so listen up. Before we begin our mission brief, I want you to check under your seats."

Mathe and I grinned at each other and did as the boss requested. The Talons ready room aboard the Raleigh was electric with

---

[1] *Commander Joe "Hoser" Satrapa suffered the loss of his right thumb and was determined to not let it stop his flying fighter aircraft. He convinced the surgeon to take off his right big toe and attach it to his right hand. Now he had three fingers and a big toe. It looked a bit like a lobster claw, but Hoser demonstrated that he could operate the trim button, so he went back on flight status...with a new call sign, "Toeser."

expectation as each aviator got up and reached down to pluck a taped Cuban cigar from under their seats.

"In another world, gentlemen, that would have been a dollar bill—and the message would have been that you have to get off your asses to make a buck. However, today—ah." He hesitated and continued.

"OK, I know you pukes think of yourselves as fighter types stuck in attack, and that is OK. Understand our work is more important to the war effort than flying around looking for someone to shoot. We have orders to do some real damage—yes, drop bombs. But our mission and all those to come might at some point require your ability to fight our enemy in the air. For those of you who might have forgotten, it's called dog fighting—ACM (Air Combat Maneuvering). So just in case you get that rare opportunity to take the shot and maybe even bag a gomer, we will be ready to pull these out, *together* and party until no one can see straight. But trust me, keep 'em safe. I'll be checking so no one jumps the gun, and when that day arrives and your smoke ain't the brand of Cuban you hold in your hand, there will be hell to pay."

"No one smokes 'em until Talons draw blood—then we all join in! Got it? Now go out and bomb the shit out of 'em! He challenged. "So who will be the first shooter?" he added, followed by his usual smirk.

"Bob, give them your strike weather brief for our target today." Kilkenny said, as he stepped aside so LT Andy Johannes could provide strike details.

Mathe leaned over to me, smiled, and whispered, "The Skipper just threw down raw meat, and someone is going to eat. What do you think?"

I grinned and winked back.

I looked down at my watch while clawing away the need for sleep—the 4 a.m. start to the Talons'day was getting old.

Another REECE —more like a search and destroy. Hunt for them, find them, and kill them quickly, I thought.

While listening to Andy's weather brief, I thought of the beautiful sunrises that had awaited us on deck at this time of day. The thrill of the launch and the concentration to get it all right is what I liked. I'd be tasked to the limit with compartmentalized procedures, the anticipation of how to save myself on a cold cat or worse, and thoughts of the climb out, headings, frequencies, section catch-up, and emergencies that could happen from startup until the final trap. I would be swimming in details—and loving it—the adrenaline and the expectation of precise airmanship.

After reaching the last step to the fight deck from the ready room, I caught the heightened energy on top. I watched the tightly ordered pre-launch deck dance. Sailors in a spectrum of colored vests—all with specific damanding tasks manuevered around each other and jets in a choatic but well choreographed dance. It is an exacting ballet performed on a rolling deck with variable winds—and it never ceased to amaze me. God, I love this shit!

Everything was different—heightened, but yet the same. It didn't matter if you wore a purple, green, red, brown, yellow, or white vest—signaling your pre-launch tasks on deck. Each sailor's face reflected earnest suspense and hard work that is war. The rest of my flight scattered and manned up to their machines while picking up each other's eyes looking to confirm support. I made direct eye contact with Jake, my plane captain, and felt the pull of him wanting to go with us. I tried to tamp down the thought that he might be my last human contact on this earth.

The excitement was contagious as I patted the yin-yang symbol on the side of my helmet twice before climbing aboard the A-4. The ancient symbol seemed out of place in this war—but my destiny today favored yin— if you believe war is negative, dark, and evil. Going medieval was what was necessary today. My ritual before manning up was always the same, but today was different. Today there would be no balance between good and bad—just total absolute destruction of whatever we could find in the jungles to the north. Anyone on the ground with a gun and some without were my bitch today.

As "Knuckles" said, "We are looking to kill something today."

After manning up to the A-4, I locked in Koch fittings to my shoulder harness and checked my COM hookup, O2 and G-suit connections to the aircraft after stowing my pulled ejection seat safety pins. Brown-shirt plane captain Jake held the outer pins, removed from the jet over his head, and I acknowledged before he stowed them. I liked Jake—trusted him.

I caught "Knuckles" Heming giving a thumbs-up (more like a toes up) to his plane captain—His bulbous thumb/toe exclamation point always gave you the feeling that he meant it. But his thumb/toe after being in his boot for all those years sure must have smelled.

Air boss Tyler Haughton's intercom words radiated throughout the ship. "Standby to start the jets."

With deck loudspeakers blaring, Jake caught my attention again with twirling fingers for my start sequence.

With Jake's turn-up signal and the start cart whining, engine RPMs rose to 15 percent. I rounded the horn with the throttle, and the airplane began to moan with life as the igniters did their job.

I pulled my head away from the checklist and out of the cockpit while searching the horizon. Yes, the deck was moving a little more than I was used to. The sea state was less than calm this morning with a heavy smell of saltwater air and a warm breeze.

I looked over at Mathe, then to Commander Al "Taco" Chavez and Ensign James "Butts" Butler. Only one in our division caught my eye and acknowledged my look. Each was deep into their pre-launch/startup procedures. Again, I glanced back at Mathe as he sat rock solid and quiet—deep in his own thoughts.

At times, Mathe was legendary in his flying precision. Who would have thought he could make the transition from choppers to jets look so easy? For him failure was not an option and drove him even harder to perform. The thought of being unworthy always nagged him.

Each pilots individualized "brain buckets" (flight helmets) caught my attention for some reason. While I waited, they brought back memories of all of the helmets I had worn for protection in my youth even though now I have more baseball caps than most stores. Each recollection of past football, lacrosse, motorcycle, bike, hockey, and skiing helmets worn brought a smile to my face. They mostly held positive memories. One incident though stuck in my mind. The scar is still there—my helmet hadn't helped much.

I was knocked colder than a mackerel in an intercity hockey game rivalry getting my lip opened up like a sardine can. I knew my current "brain bucket" wouldn't stop a 20mm bullet or any bullet for that matter from penetrating my gourd. It was only designed to keep me awake if my head bounced off the canopy—giving its owners a false sense of protection. Realistically, it offered no real protection against what we might run into this morning.

Errant temperature and pressure gage hiccups finally woke me from my helmet daydream and told me something wasn't right with the jet. I hand-signaled my plane captain, alerting him that my jet was down, "on hold," and I needed time to troubleshoot the problem.

"Boss, 010 ready to go in two minutes," I called, as I cycled and troubleshot the likely culprit.

I then caught Taco and then Mathe on the port cat shoot off the bow one after the other—and I was left sitting there fucking up the flight deck launch sequence. What the hell. Just as the deck troubleshooter plugged his COM plug into the side of my jet and tapped his ear, indicating "I want to talk," the errant instrument reading jumped into the bottom of the green. I looked down at him and signaled I was ready.

The deck plane director aggressively got my attention as I refocused, and he taxied me forward. His body language and facial expression told it all—he was not happy with the trouble I had caused with his launch flow. *Fuck it!* I thought. What I didn't know was that Ensign Butts was having his own problems, and now our two-man section launch was not going to happen—a highly irregular move. I guess they figured they could get Butts off the deck in time to complete the form-up for our division attack.

The deck crew eased me into the shuttle, and the catapult officer gave me his baton (flashlight with a plastic cone attached) in the air twirl signal for me to go to full power—impatient to blow me off the ship after my hold. With full power the jet was straining against the holdback, ready to leap forward. I flipped the wingtip lights on—signaling my readiness to launch. As I wiped out the cockpit with the stick for confirmation that the jet's control surfaces were free and clear, I planted my head against the ejection seat, grabbed the catapult flip-down grip, and cupped my right hand behind the stick. Out of the corner of my eye on my left, I caught the yellow-shirted CAT (catapult) officer swing his arm forward and drop to one knee while touching the deck with his light baton—a signal for the shooter to blow me off the deck. As I shot down the CAT and off the bow, I felt the familiar and inevitable float then sink, and eased my thoughts away from the ejection handle.

Immediately, I caught the sink with a slight backward stick, confirmed full power and the vertical speed indicator going in the right direction—up. I checked the RAT (Ram Air Turbine) position lever one more time in case of electrical loss, smacked the gear handle up, and pulled flaps up while cutting across the bow of the ship and immediately into the goo gaining altitude. I found Mathe, but Taco just disappeared in the clouds while Butts was left twiddling his fingers, back on the boat—over whatever. He had downed his aircraft.

"Where the hell is that guy?" I cursed as I took flight lead back from Mathe. " A three-plane division—great! But the skipper's words, "Bomb the shit out of 'em," grabbed my attention again.

Seventeen: Stitched

The Fuzz Buster Save
"Paint It Black" – Rolling Stones

Mathe and I finally found Taco, then all three of us went to work and "bombed the shit out of them" as ordered. Mission accomplished.

The bomb run over a not-too-visible truck park brought significant secondary fire and debris plumes (fuel or ordnance) that rose high in the humid jungle air—a rarity in this no-nothing, can't-find-a-real-target ground attack war.

But, as I egressed the target I wondered if Mathe and Taco had left the bomb run without difficulty. I did not know that both Mathe and Taco had flown through a bomb debris cloud. And I had lost sight of them prior to the join up for the flight back to the boat.

Mathe and Taco searched the empty sky to locate their flight lead Finn—to no avail.

My heart pounded wildly as I realized I had a problem—and it was mine alone. The A-4's response to control stick inputs gave me no reassurance that she would fly much longer. I scanned my port wing and caught the partially-deployed battle-damaged wing slat. *Ah, what the fuck!*

Over the target the aft end of my Skyhawk sounded like it had been hit multiple times but I wasn't really sure. I kept my eyes glued to the gauges, expecting the worst. Then the side of the cockpit exploded inward and I felt immediate numbness in my face and rear end. The gomers had nailed me, and the jet's unresponsiveness told the whole story. The last ribbon of ground tracer (AAA) fire had pounded my jet—and good.

Suddenly, my entire emergency warning panel lit up like a rainbow.

Jesus! I am in some serious shit.

The knot in my stomach got tighter and I fought back with well-trained procedures to save myself and the jet—but the pain kept grabbing me. After losing my flight, I was alone in a very hostile territory—limping home to the boat.

As I struggled with my heavily damaged A-4 and I realized this was now all about survival. My intent had been to rendezvous with a tanker before landing on the carrier. But, I knew my wounds and aircraft would dictate another story. I was in real trouble.

I listened to the communist search radars and turned my IFF to emergency. I then made my "feet wet" call at the coastal egress point on my way out of northern Vietnam.

"Playboy" gave me the hand off to "Sea Biscuit."

Sea Biscuit— a Navy E-1 Tracer was quarterbacking the strike today. He was looking for MiGS, monitoring airwing assets and preventing friendly fire engagements.

Finn keyed his mic button, "Claw 1, over."

"Claw 1, go ahead, Sea Biscuit," responded the airborne controller.

"Have significant battle damage—declaring an emergency—descending through FL 270 on a heading of one three zero degrees—request a steer to the nearest tanker."

"Claw 1, we will relay. Your steer to the ship is one four zero degrees."

I made the correction adjustment to my TACAN needle and waited for it to lock into the ship.

Another guage check and I saw my low fuel state.

"Jesus, Bingo fuel. Where is the fucking tanker?"

What I didn't know was that Taco and Mathe, part of my division on the strike, were also finding their way back to the boat when they heard my call to Sea Biscuit.

* * *

Finn's mayday startled both. They immediately contacted the airborne controller "Sea Biscuit" for a steer to intercept Finn's flight path. They were relieved that Finn was still in the game motoring for the boat—but his emergency transmissions were now a big concern.

"There he is, Taco, on your nose, five right—low," Mathe stammered.

Finn's aircraft seemed to be wallowing in the air. Was he wounded or was it aircraft damage that was causing his jet to wing walk and stagger in his descent? Finn was erratic, and the liquid flying smoothness he was known for was anything but that right now. His pixie-dust excellence was nowhere to be found.

After joining up on Finn's wing, Mathe immediately noticed Finn's shattered windscreen and errant slat and pressed his COM button. *What a mess*, he thought, as his eyes poured over his friend's heavily damaged fighter.

"Finn, you OK?" he called.

No answer.

"Hey, Finn, the cavalry has arrived. How are you doing?" Mathe said matter-of-factly.

"Good to see you bone heads. Got, got, got—ssssome problems," Finn acknowledged.

Noting Finn's cotton-mouth tension and torn-up jet, Mathe called, "Finn, try and keep your heading and descent rate steady while I pass under you—to check you out."

Finn double tapped his mic button to acknowledge.

Finn's damaged radio calls were as irregular as his slurred speech. Mathe offered encouragement as he passed under Claw 1 to confirm damage. Suddenly, Taco's radio call stepped all over Mathe's calls to Finn.

"Boys, we got company," Taco shouted. "Just got strobed at five o'clock—any of you getting lit up?"

With a push of adrenaline Mathe immediately swiveled away from the mess that was Finn's aircraft in a search for the source of the transmissions. He said to himself, *Jesus we're getting spiked, I gotta to take this guy out before he gets a shot off.*

Mathe knew Taco's call was more alarming than Finn's emergency as it upped the threat for all of them.

Taco and Mathe pulled away in combat spread while Mathe tightened his harness straps as tight as he could take it. They turned their IFFs (friend or foe identification) to standby—no transmission for friend or foe could be picked up now. But the search radar emissions from the higher tone enemy radar kept penetrating their ears and concentration.

Mathe lowered his nose two degrees while continuing to push the PCL (throttle) forward to pick up speed for the pull-away from Finn—with Taco in trail and he pressed his mic button.

"Taco, give Sea Biscuit a quick peek at us, with an IFF flash, and make the call to verify the contact one more time," Mathe commanded.

Taco acknowledged with two mic clicks.

Before Taco could depress his COM button he heard, "Claw Flight, this is Sea Biscuit. We confirm an unidentified monitored aircraft, suspected hostile, at your eight o'clock, closing forty miles, Angels seventeen and climbing."

* * *

Back on board the Raleigh, "Alert 5," with Lieutenant "Shaka" White and Lieutenant Commander "Tilly" Tilden were monitoring Claw flight's communications over their COM's discrete channel in the cockpit of their F-4. They were beyond ready to jump into the fight and they couldn't believe they hadn't been launched to provide CAP support.

In his mind, Shaka was giving the air boss what for. *Shoot me off this fucking deck and let me give Finn some good old-fashioned CAP. I want to blast the commie back to the MiG's production plant in the USSR.* They both knew that their Phantom was loaded "for bear" and would be more than an equalizer for Claw flight and Claw 1.

Shaka grabbed his dangling O2 mask hanging off the side of his helmet and pulled it over his sweat soaked face to speak, shouting in his mind, *Damn it, boss, we're only seconds away in burner—launch us!*

Shaka hesitated, for the second time, through the aggression that was dripping down his face and pounded the F-4's canopy rail. "Boss, we're up and ready to go" No answer. Shaka and Tilly stewed in frustration, while listening to Claw flight, knowing they could make a difference—if they could just get the fuck off the boat!

* * *

"Mathe, have you got your fuzz buster radar unit with you? You know, the one Rusty sent you from Radio Shack, cause I'm not picking up that unidentified," Taco said.

"Hold one, Taco, bringing it online as we speak. Nice. It's functioning better than our on board stuff.

"Taco, you stay with Finn—go combat spread, high right in a quartering trail. I'll get the lock and greet our new friend," Mathe commanded.

"Take a 160-degree heading and get him home for God's sake."

As Mathe broke from the formation to engage the bogey he glanced back and noticed Finn's aircraft was trailing fuel into the slipstream.

Taco thought he had a bit of time, so he joined Finn to give some reassurance and to look him over before preparing for the covering spread. Taco could not believe what he saw. Multiple rounds had passed right through the cockpit, grazing Finn's face, shredding his O2 mask, while taking out the console.

Finn felt the dampness of his flight suit and hoped it reflected only sweat. It covered the lower half of his body—and might be telling another story. He could feel himself going in and out of consciousness. Not a good sign!

Mathe cobbed the throttle and instantly felt his G-suit expand to counteract the g-load in a fast stable level right turn. Breathing deeply, he fumbled with his fuzz buster radar unit while pushing the throttle to a high cruise power setting and finished his combat checkoffs. He was sweating profusely as he eyeballed the sky ahead, searching for the hostel.

He flipped on the IFF momentarily again to give Sea Biscuit a read on their position and immediately turned it to standby.

"Claw 3, your bandit is now at twenty-five miles, FL240, off your nose and climbing," Sea Biscuit warned.

Mathe acknowledged by keying his mic and confirmed the bandit's location with his civilian fuzz buster turned MiG-killing radar. He was not flying 010, the inherited Marine A-4M with RAW (airborne radar) on this strike, so the fuzz buster was part of the answer if they were to survive. Radio Shack would be proud of their contribution to the war effort!

Time to shoot first now and worry about the consequences later, Mathe thought.

"Christ, it works, Taco—got a good paint on the asshole."

"Hang in there, Finn. Mathe has this guy—keep working your problem—and try to hold a 160-degree heading to the ship. Go to button six; we have a ready deck. I'm covering you high right," Taco could be heard saying.

Taco eased his A-4 into a high perch position while monitoring Finn's progress.

Taco's words of encouragement helped, but Finn knew it was all up to him to get the crippled A-4 back on board the Raleigh. Between the execution of procedures to save his A-4 and himself from the battle damage, he wondered how Mathe was doing on the intercept—protecting them from the bogey. Mathe had a fist for a heart—confidence in himself—and today was no different. This was the real thing, and Mathe wasn't flying a CH-46 for the Corps.

I'm glad he's with us!

Mathe had the bandit IDed but realized he had few problems of his own now.

"No missiles on this attack mission, bomb load dropped, just two guns—against a MiG. Are you kidding me?" Mathe mumbled to himself. *If I fly the shit out of this thing, maybe I get this guy and go home, too. No choice here. Have to protect my boys.*

Sweat was draining out from under his helmet into his eyes, and his Nomex flight suit felt like he had just come out of the swimming pool during water survival.

"Claw 3, we have a missile launch from the bogey, now off your nose and level at ten miles and closing. Sea Biscuit, over."

Into The Fight

Mathe found the missile track with his handheld cop detector.

"Roger, Claw 3," he responded.

Mathe's jet was at one hundred percent when he finally caught the metallic fuselage reflection of his target—making the turn and coming hard with an incredible closure rate. His abdominals tensed as he tried to hold his jet's vibrating airframe steady.

He had spotted the missile coming off the MiG's wing rail—right for him.

Combat checklist complete—mill settings for the gun site—maybe just like a ground straffing run but easier and Jesus scarier. This was real! He steadied and leveled the jet with his nose directly on the rapidly closing MiG's missile.

Two guns versus one crazy gomer with a considerble advantage—I should probably be running from this guy, he thought.

Hold the heading until the last minute and pull hard away to lose the missile lock, he remembered. *Some evasive tactic, now that my life is on the line.*

Save the flight, Mathe. Concentrate. They don't have a chance if you don't shoot this gomer.

Finally, a Marine attack pilot in an aerial duel—a gunfight, not like fighter types—just flying around looking for something to shoot, but a real opportunity right in front of me. No sidewinders, just a gun "for defense only," they told me. Oh, what the hell.

Stay on task! It's stick, rudder, and eyeball time.

While centering the gun sight reticules before squeezing the trigger, Mathe unconsciously tried to tuck his shoulders into his ears while bracing for the oncoming missile's impact.

Waiting to the last minute for the missle to close on him, he then slammed the stick sideways, rolled the jet inverted, and pulled hard, punching out flares in a Hail Mary maneuver to beat it. As his A-4 passed through the horizon nose down and arcing 180 degrees, the altimeter whipped counter-clockwise quickly by FL250, 230, 220, while he reversed course to face the threat again—missiles or MiG.

The MiG's missile overshot and flew by his canopy—which seemed like 10 feet away. Quickly, Mathe felt and heard a massive explosion followed by what sounded like a mass of marbles hitting his jet. The ensuing buffet forced the A-4's nose to yaw dramatically to port as his head bounced laterally off the canopy.

"This guy is serious! Two ATOLLs fired and I didn't even see the second. The son-of-a-bitch is going to pay for that," Mathe fumed.

The second missile that exploded off Mathe's tail had done its job—now *he* was also in trouble.

Pitch control was compromised and the three emergency lights on his instrument panel told the story as the MiG flew by on a direct course—hunting Finn and Taco.

"Got to keep this jet flying," he muttered.

He took one more scan of the instruments and pulled hard left, five degrees nose low, and felt reasonable initial controllability. He continued the pull in the direction of the MiG while grunting into the G-suit, to keep the blood in his head and upper body from draining out—and not passing out.

The A-4 would have no part of his high-speed G pull this time and broke into an early stall. He released the pull, unloading the airplane, and she found her air and was flying again—but just barely. She still had teeth. He finally made the turn and pushed her for more speed. Add two more warning/emergency lights—system compromises—to the mix.

The sight of Finn's jet flashed in his mind. *Hope they are OK. They probably think I've gunned this fucker by now.*

Keep it together, "Rock," Got to get to Finn and Taco.

In hot low-trail pursuit he knew his "Amigos" had no idea what was in store for them as the MiG closed in on them from the west.

Mathe's thumb found the COM button on the throttle and warned, "Hey, Taco, the MiG just blew by me and is hard after you guys. I called Sea Biscuit and asked for immediate fighter support again. Man, we need them now!"

Trying to calm himself and keep his emotions in check, he shouted, "What's Finn's status?"

* * *

Finn didn't know it, but he was flying a perfect section lead—even with his difficulties and stuck wing slat. Taco rode Finn's wing in their direct course to the carrier. He relayed progress reports while encouraging Finn to cover the checklists and prepare for ejection. Even though Claw 1 went Bingo fuel (low fuel/divert), Finn's hallucinating calculations indicated the possibility of a rendezvous with the tanker that had been launched from the ship.

Finn continued to descend through FL 270 in his heavily damaged A-4 fighter.

"Got to get gas—Bingo fuel, shit—and get back to the carrier," he mumbled.

Finn's tried to clear his mind to deal with the priorities that Claw 1 was dictating. He was in and out of consciousness from his injuries and fought to stay in the right now—in the game. With each new warning light in the cockpit, his concerns grew. He was boiling in mental sweat as waves of fear swept over him with each drop of lost blood.

His shot-up fighter was somehow still manageable, but concern about making it back to the boat overrode his caution about placing the tanker in jeopardy with his increasing lack of control.

"And now a MiG on our tail—great!"

"Claw flight, your bogey is on a 160-degree bearing, at 20 miles and climbing. We have two F-4s on an intercept, forty out—but it will be tight, Sea Biscuit."

"Roger—Claw 1," Finn slowly responded.

"God, where is everyone?"

"Taco, this is Mathe. You still go high and wide for the deflection when the gomer shows—he will most likely go for Finn." *He's slow, trailing fuel with a jet that is a wreck—that MiG can't miss? Maybe he will go for Taco?*

God, am I setting my buddy up as bait—fuel contrail and all? Mathe wondered.

"I'm still searching for you, Taco. I should be closing from your 180 low and fast for the intercept. Got a few problems from the exploding missile off my tail—but my guns still function. Let's trap this prick quick," said Mathe. "Got anything bigger to fight with than a 20mm?"

"No sidewinders today on our load-outs, pard—we're going to have to gun this guy if he shows," Taco said.

"OK, Taco. Let's Thatch (aerial combat tactic) him up then."

"Mathe, I got you low off my starboard wing—keep your turn and climb coming." Out of the corner of Mathe's eye, he caught the MiG already lined up to take his boys out. Why was the MiG waiting?

Mathe was out of time and out of range—no shot at this distance! While pulling hard into the MiG, Mathe reefed a load of 20mm off his nose, hoping to divert his attention. The MiG would have nothing of it and continued his pursuit of Mathe's two squids. Time was running out.

Mathe tightened the pull. If the jet lost it completely, so be it. He then reefed off another load of 20mm into thin air, trying to force a confrontation—a turn into him. That was it, 400 rounds gone, and the gomer, not to be deterred, continued his lineup on Finn.

What Mathe didn't see was Taco on the perch putting his pipper (optical gun sight) in the sight a fraction ahead of the MiG. Taco pulled the trigger and unloaded an arc of slugs into the gomer's machine—just as two F-4s passed just above Mathe's canopy in full burner looking for glory.

The MiG's fuselage twinkled like a Christmas tree and then belched an explosive discharge of smoke from the aft end of the jet with chunks of fuselage sprinkling the sky— into the slipstream. That was it, Mathe thought, as the MiG-21 made its last turn in a black streaming contrail dive.

This is Taco's kill today, could have been mine—sorry fellas. Mucho Gracious Amigo!

"Thanks for your help today Tiger flight—you guys have trouble getting off the boat? Claw 3,"Mathe called sarcastically. They didn't miss a beat except his meaning.

"Roger, Claw 3. Anytime we can be of service. We'll cover you back to the Raleigh."

What were they thinking? Euchred out of a kill by a savvy attack pilot? Pissed we were doing their job for them today?I hoped! Combat Air Patrol, my ass!

"Oh, by the way, nice shooting," Wolf 1 hesitantly called.

Each word was oozing jealousy, as the two F-4s reversed and swung high and wide behind to cover Claw flight's exit.

While trying to stabilize his bird, Mathe limped up into the flight on Taco's right wing and gave him some distance in his loose "shotgun" join-up.

Mathe was excited about Taco's success and yet concerned that his systems failures would force his jet to depart its flight envelope. No fire, no loss of fuel. Just shot-up control surfaces, Mathe surmised. *Hell, I was broken yet golden, maybe,* he thought.

"Taco, it's your lead. You got the heading? Not bad shooting for a Navy man—killer! You've got two beat-up birds to lead home," Mathe said.

"Mathe, what is your fuel state? We're vectored for the onboard tanker that was just launched. Finn is losing fuel fast and is down to .8."

"Low state, Taco," Mathe mumbled before he called, "1.8."

* * *

Taco spotted the converted A-4 tanker and called, "Claw 2 with a flight of three for a plug."

He watched the refueling store (Buddy Store) on Hose 4, carried on the center-line rack below the tanker, begin reeling out the 50 feet of refueling hose with a drogue.

Hose 4 glanced, to port and was amazed at what he saw: Two A-4s in the flight were holed out, flack damage with smoking bullet holes, significant structural damage, and fuel streaming out of one at an alarming rate. The first machine in the tanking evolution was barely holding it together—a damaged, partially deployed slat was causing controllability problems.

The tanker pilot could see the canopy was partially destroyed, and the pilot was having his problems flying his battle-damaged, beat-up machine as Finn approached. *This guy must be working his ass off for the lineup, he thought.* He hesitated for just a second out of concern for the safety of this flight but quickly came to his senses—*Got to help my squadron mate now!*

"Try to hold your optimum AOA," Hose 4 coached.

Mathe's attention was diverted from his problems to that of his buddy. *Oh, brother, make this easy for Finn—he could flame at any second,*

"OK, Claw flight, drogue out," Hose 4 called.

"Finn, you're up first. Ease on over to the tanker. Mathe, give us some separation while you sort things out," said Taco. They continued in level echelon.

"Bring it on in Claw 1. You know the lineup—form left, plug center, reform right," called Hose 4.

"Wolf flight, hold off until we complete Claw flight's evolution."

"Roger, Wolf 1."

They pulled into a loosely stacked echelon to wait for their tanking sequence and cooled their heels in frustrated jealousy—tempered by their concern for the shot-up A-4s.

The basket was dancing, but Finn didn't flinch as he drove his receiver into the drogue on the first pass. With his wounds and the aircraft's damage Mathe was amazed that without chasing the basket he speared it in one attempt and got a green transfer signal. But his flying was still erratic though. He doubted that Finn's partially deployed errant slat was totally responsible his jet's instability. *Maybe his wounds were catching up to him?*

Again the cockpit began swirling and everything for Finn abruply turned black. With only 1.3 pounds of fuel aboard his battle-damaged jet, Finn abruptly fell away from the tanker and staggered away from the flight—not enough to get home. Coming back to consciousness again, Finn scanned his instruments, trying to concentrate. The overpowering feeling of wanting to rest was working its magic. Perspiring profusely and fighting to stay awake, he knew any letdown in concentration could be suicidal. As he turned away from the flight and found his course to the Raleigh, he concentrated on keeping control of his jet. He knew he was in real trouble—he was afraid.

He could hear Taco and Mathe's radio calls of encouragement on and off as he slipped into darkness again.

Eighteen: Face Curtain Calls

Riding the Rails
"Chain of Fools" – Aretha Franklin

The throbbing in Mathe's forearm continued, from an early childhood accident—an old injury that he never reported to the Navy. Squeezing his thighs together to hold the stick, brought some relief. He could rest his arm for a few seconds. Just as he was dialing the tactical squadron's assigned frequency with his other hand, he noticed Finn's jet wobble again.

What he didn't know but suspected was that Finn was losing blood from his wounds as he watched Finn's descent and the rapidly decaying control of his aircraft.

The wind racing by his canopy brought Finn back from his temporary dream state, on his letdown to the boat off the coast. He couldn't hold onto consciousness and wondered if he was bleeding out. Had Mathe's calls brought him back?

"Hold it together, buddy. We're almost home," called Mathe, as he watched the fuel stream drain out of Finn's aircraft.

* * *

Finn tried to keep his head up. Holding onto hope, he took a glance at the gauges to reconfirm his problems. He felt the energy getting sucked out of his machine and himself and pressed his mic button. As he held onto hope, his fingers found the appropriate buttons and knobs inside the cockpit to fight his emergencies—but he knew he was rapidly succumbing.

"Mathe, not sure I can stretch this glide to the boat," he said, trying to sound confident.

Finn slowly rolled the "scooter" towards shore, thinking that his chances for survival were better over land. He was just a step into the North, and he would find a way out into the safety of the south. Blood in the water on an ejection was the last thing he wanted after hearing stories of aggressive shark populations off the shoreline. Finn's mind raced.

He continued to stare out of the cockpit into the empty sky ahead and felt as if he was not here. The amber lights in front of him suddenly meant less as he sank further into his seat. He was more than scared and trying to get smaller with each minute so that no one would touch him, not even the jet. Time seemed to compress as he held the stick a little tighter and alternated between accepting his fate and fighting for his life.

For a moment he seemed to be processing everything faster than possible—faster than actual events were happening in front of him. Then blackness—then back again with a jerk of his head.

Don't take the easy way out, Finn—work to survive. You have support; the ship is waiting for you. Taco and Mathe are on your wing—you will make it. But then…

The Engine Fire Warning Light suddenly blinked intermittently and then glared full- on from Finn's instrument panel—and told it all.

"My God—fire! God, no—not today, not now— please!" Finn yelled.

As he heard the crackle of hot metal from the rear of the airplane and felt the heat rising, a small wisp of smoke rose from the cockpit floor. The jet seemed to jump, and suddenly he was watching the dirt and everything else on the cockpit floor rise to his eye level—and just as suddenly drop. It only took a second.

Holding on for dear life, he yelled, "I need more fuel now, but fire, no, no, no." Claw 1 stalled and fell further away from the tanker.

He fought for control, held the stick tighter, and squeezed her even harder—to get the attention she was not giving him, to control her, to fight her if he had to. But she then yawed into a rapidly decaying roll/ spin. The fog bank below was about to swallow both of them, and he continued to strain and yell at her to give him control.

He was in a survival vice, holding onto life and fighting the opportunity to leave. *Eject before it is too late,* he told himself. Mathe and Taco's voices were screaming at him to punch out—but he held on for a little more distance—ever closer to the Raleigh, he thought.

He blacked out again for a moment as the jet departed flight again and began to tumble. His jet was now flying backward—a true ass-ender on his hands. Heat startled him awake.

"Please, God, get the nose to come around, out of the flame, so that I can leave," he cried.

The hot rod slowly began to turn its nose toward the fog bank— down. Thoughts ran through his mind.

"Forget the wounds and pain and saving the A-4—this goes deeper than that," he mumbled.

A calm took over Finn—nothing mattered much to him now. Neither the pain in his groin and cheek, the heat and fire; not the locker room/cockpit smell of leather oil, jet fuel, sweat, the dry, rubbery on-demand O2 he breathed nor wind whistling through the holes underneath and right beside him. Outside what was left of his canopy he saw Mathe frantically giving him hand signals flying next to him—someone yelling for him to eject.

"Finn, Get out! Get out of the airplane, now!" Mathe yelled.

Finn just didn't care anymore—as the fire crept further forward into the body of his jet.

Trying to remain calm and cool-headed with some sort of control, he muttered, "Ah, here we go."

* * *

Mathe took a glance over at Finn and caught what he thought was the last gasp of Claw 1.

The aft end of Finn's jet was now fully aflame as Mathe and Taco pulled away from their squadron mate, as the possibility sunk in of what might happen to their aircraft if the worst happened to Finn.

What is Finn waiting for? Mathe thought, in a panic.

Mathe watched his squadron mate and best friend get swallowed up and disappear into the fog below. Finn's calls were less frequent now but more urgent as Mathe lost sight of him.

Finn was utterly gone, out of sight—into the weather that was hugging the atmoshere above the ground—just inside the border of North Vietnam.

Mathe, at 2,000 feet on his radio altimeter, caught his descent rate with power—almost 85 percent, and then a scooch more. He added a touch of back stick while trimming out the stick forces to hold the angle of attack at 15 units in a constant-rate turn—and began circling the area where Finn had disappeared. He was shaking uncontrollably—

mad as hell—for losing his friend. He continued his circle of the area in the hope that Finn would come up on his COM. He knew that the fog bank was not supposed to dissipate soon, which meant little likelihood of a rescue operation. He had to do something.

In full anger, and shaking from the loss of his buddy, he yelled at himself, "Goddamnit, get your ass in gear! You can save Finn."

Finn's jet flipped again into a nose-over tailpipe tumble while descending—which brought the fire suddenly over the canopy and then just as suddenly away. Then again—fire, no fire—a thundering, groaning vibration and then the cycle of flame, then no flame. The jet was tearing itself apart and Finn with it.

His dad's experience suddenly flashed in his mind.

* * *

Doc leveled us at 7,500 feet, dropped the gear, and opened the bomb bay doors to slow "Starduster" down while we unhooked flak vests, unplugged COM links, donned parachutes, grabbed what we could, and found our way to our respective exits.

I thought about my pilot hatch, jettisonable window, for a moment but found my way to the nose wheel well. I jumped and followed my crew members toward the cloud deck below.

We passed through the cloud deck with good chutes and descended toward the largest lake I think I had ever seen in China—so no life vests—great!

* * *

Can't save her—I have to get out of this thing before I hit the ground, Finn thought. Looking up but down—*airplane inverted—*patches of land had started to appear below the fog. Finn was suddenly worrying again about getting it all right as he tried to hold the stick steady. He threw his head back one more time—NOW! Time to go! Even though he couldn't see out of his right eye, he found the canopy jettison handle to his right and pulled.

With the aircraft still inverted, nose down, Finn grabbed the lower Escapac ejection seat handle. It was the only thing that he seemed to be able to control now and pulled—pulled hard. All he remembered on leaving the airplane was Mathe's voice and then a sucking sound and full body blast after the canopy jettisoned.

"Just let me make it through the next maneuver," Finn murmured.

Suddenly, Finn was rocketed sideways, free from the heat, into the moisture-laden fog—and then upward. He was now free, tumbling in the seat—free from the fire. The pain and concerns of flying the jet, they were all falling away. *Safe for a moment—a second,* Finn thought. He released a long held breath.

* * *

Mathe caught just a wisp of Finn's hot jet. A shadowed light reflected off the fog bank below with a sudden aura of eerie brilliance breaking away from the main ball of firelight.

Too late.

Mathe's sense of rage and duty made him realize that he could somehow save this situation—he had the knowledge and training. He just needed the right tools.

Nineteen: Sucking River Mud

"Run Through the Jungle" – Creedence Clearwater Revival

Apprehension gripped Finn as he realized something was not right.

The seat's movement through the air slowed and stabilized horizontally and just as quickly impacted something hard as Finn lost consciousness. The feeling of freshwater flowing over his hand, wrist, and then his whole arm woke him. He saw his hand laying next to him partially covered in mud on the river bottom—as if it wasn't his—unsure of everything.

"Whoa, where am I? What's happening?" he muttered.

He felt the water rising and falling, lapping at his body, almost over his mask and helmet—he was sweating, panicked and soaked.

"What the hell—I'm still in the seat?" he gasped. "God, I feel awful—have to find help."

As the pain started to envelop him—and the water continued its rise—his breathing came shallow and fast

"Drowning on a riverbank in Vietnam in this stinking war—not in this river and not today," he vowed.

"Why am I laying on my side—still in the seat, in the water? Not right," he asked himself, trying to logic himself out of the situation.

"Everything is horizontal. No seat separation? Seat malfunction? Too low for a zero-zero ejection?" he growled. "WTF?"

Confused, he realized he was still clipped, still strapped in the ejection seat on a riverbank—laying on his side, half in and half out of the water—and it was rising. He grabbed his helmet to release the O2 mask, but his right wrist rebelled in pain. He looked over—like an out-of-body-experience—his wrist and arm dangling, broken, useless by his side, laying visible in the shallow river edge beside him.

He willed himself to escape the panic that set in and vowed not to let the water take him.

Coughing and spurting water, he grabbed the shrapnel-shredded O2 mask release, with his left hand, on the side of the helmet and then tore it off—both mask and helmet in one motion. With more struggle came the release of the harness/Koch fittings—and he fell facedown in the river's ooze while sucking up a mouthful. He spit it out and got his first whiff of moist, rotten, stinking jungle. The sound of his own wretching while gasping for air—brought him back to some sense of self-consciousness.

He lay there exhausted, trying to collect himself—half in, half out of consciousness in the cool river water—peering up the river's bank for the enemy. In the next instant, he felt severe screaming pain in his groin and face and more.

Suddenly, Finn remembered a war story form his AOC training days. Gunnery Abruzzo's morbid war tale crept back into his thoughts—like a memory he wanted to forget:

* * *

The vision of dead and mutilated Vietcong bodies killed by my DI in Endoc swam across my mind. He remembers—as he glanced at the

148

DI's Vietcong kill pictures on his desk—and braces even harder. Gunny catches my eyes staring and immediately commands, "Yes, candidate, those are the dead, mutilated bodies of the enemy. They were responsible for the deaths of Sergeant Jolly, a good Marine, and many others. They deserved what they got, and I carry pictures of their dead bodies not only to honor my men that died but for the grit these little warriors displayed in the fight to survive our vengeance." Those little commie bastards were worth killing.

Remember when you get over to the Nam they will fight you with the same zeal we felt in attacking them—they will show no mercy as they try to kill you. Be prepared!

* * *

Looking like a salamander wriggling out of its primordial sludge, Finn slithered up the bank to lush green. "God, it hurts, everything hurts—face, groin, wrist, back—what's left?" Finn murmured and promptly lost consciousness, again. Awakening sometime later, he searched for his handheld "Prick 90" survival radio and pushed "Airforce Common" signal 243.

"Claw flight, this is Claw one. Anyone up?" A second and a third time.

There was no reply, but the roar of one of his squadron mate's jets circling above gave him hope. He tried to catch his breath from the unrelenting pain his body was dictating before he passed out again.

"Finn, it's Mathe. We will get to you—hang tight, pal," Mathe transmitted.

* * *

Mathe had picked up Finn's seat pack SAR beeper signal before it cut out completely. He circled the area one last time before departing for the boat and started to work the scenarios to help save his shipmate. He had enough fuel to reach the boat. His damage was not interfering with controllability—yet.

A hung bomb story might give him his out. They won't let me come aboard the Raleigh with a "hanger" so divert to, let's see, Chu Lai?— as he checked his navigation options. No, Da Nang was his best hope, with ready-made HML helo squadrons stationed close by at the Marble Mountain Marine airbase. He could borrow, more like cumshaw, a Huey for Finn's rescue. His old squadron was still stationed there he hoped.

* * *

All I wanted was my chance to punch some American-hating zealot in the kisser, and I end up passed out, bleeding, and coughing up mud on the bank of some river in Vietnam—WTF, Finn thought.

As he peered over the river's berm and spread the high elephant grass apart, Finn noticed movement in the shadows under the dark forest canopy beyond. As he looked for a way to escape, the grassy, flat plateau to the south that paralleled the river caught his attention. He knew he had to leave, but the struggle to rise was too much, so he quietly crawled back to the ejection seat, pried the survival seat pan out, and slipped back into the river mud.

The current collected and swept him away as he tried to hold on to reality and the seat pack holding his emergency gear.

In time, he remembered hands grabbing and lifting him away from the water—the humidity so thick it was choking him. And, God the pain. He didn't want to move. He knew he was seriously injured.

In and out of consciousness again, he remembered periodic caresses of his wounds, poking, and pinpricks in all the wrong places, and intense emotional conversations in Vietnamese.

He found ways to hide his consciousness until his surroundings told him whether they supported him or if he was now a prisoner of war.

He woke to find himself on a ratan mat that covered a dirt floor—with light filtering thru the walls. He could smell not only his odor but the unmistakable stink of the river. With his left, hand, he searched for his radio transmitter. More than a battle hangover this day, he really felt bad, and the smell of feces and blood only made things worse.

His body felt as if it had been beaten with a baseball bat. He was in pain everywhere and unsure of which part of his body to move first—as he slowly took stock of his surroundings.

The stare of a mama-san tending a small cooking fire across from him caused him to pause. Her emotionless stone face glanced at him without murmuring a word. *What does she have in store for me?* he wondered.

He could hold it no more—he had to pee, and so he struggled to lift his pain-wracked upper body.

Finn caught the malevolent stare of the little peasant woman, then noticed he was in a doorless thatched hut. Surprisingly she helped him up. And with her assistance, they moved outside. He was met with roaming pigs, stray barking dogs, and irritated stares. As he struggled through the humidity and mud, the odor of the jungle was overpowering, and he welcomed a return to the hut.

His pain came in waves but he knew one certainty—he had to get out of there for his extraction as he patted his body to locate his survival radio. He remembered a plateau as they carried him from the riverbank to the village? It couldn't be far.

* * *

As Mathe formulated his plan he radioed Taco.

"Taco, call Sea Biscuit. They can notify RESCAP for Finn's pickup—I'll provide Finn's fix. I'm wrestling with a misbehaving, shot-up engine from the MiG's missile and I need to get this jet on the ground. I can make Da Nang if she holds together. Tell Strike I have a hung bomb and severe battle damage." *This just might work.*

Taco turned to look at Mathe's ordnance issue. He knew Mathe already had a plan ready for Finn's rescue—they'd dropped any ordinance they had long ago.

"Roger, Mathe, what's up? You got a plan?

Mathe smiled and answered, "Better yet, Taco, you make that call to Sea Biscuit and then head for the boat. I'll call Strike and tell them of our situation and you follow up for your approach and landing instructions. Good shooting today, Taco. You saved our asses."

Taco answered with two clicks to confirm Mathe's call. He was caught between the pure joy of shooting the MiG and seriously sad for the loss of Finn.

After Taco notified Sea Biscuit, Mathe called Raleigh (Hawk) approach. "Hawk approach, Claw 3 is up."

"Roger, Claw 3. We have you. Hawk approach."

"Claw 3 requests divert to Da Nang with significant battle damage. Claw 2 will contact you for approach and landing instructions in ten. Sea Biscuit has been notified that claw 1 is down."

"Claw 3, if unable to report upon landing for overhead at 7:00 contact us immediately—and good luck sir."

However, Mathe's real concern centered around getting back to his shipmate Finn—a personal rescue. He knew that the ground fog might not dissipate to allow air protection or a direct rescue chopper into

Finn's position. It was now his responsibility to save his buddy even though he knew it would cost him. What the hell—he'd been there before. Land at Da Nang and hump over to the Marine airfield at Marble Mountain—just southeast of Da Nang. It was an active station for Marine rescue and attack helo squadrons.

"Claw 1, Claw 3 on guard. You with me?" Mathe continued to make calls to Finn on the emergency frequency in the hope his buddy would respond—but nothing.

Twenty: The Kamikaze Save

"We Gotta Get Out of This Place" – Animals

"Claw 3—you copy, Claw 2?" Taco called.

"Claw 3 copies loud and clear," Mathe replied.

"No immediate RESCAP for Finn. They were all weathered in. Forecasters are not optimistic of significant weather changes in their reports but are actively monitoring for transmissions from Claw 1. Air cover has been notified and will be available if needed when the weather clears in the area. Claw 2 out."

Mathe switched channels and made the call to Da Nang Approach Control. He was told to squawk his IFF for his clearance into this highly active military airspace. Approach gave him a series of corrected steers to the field at about 40 miles out and ordered him to contact Da Nang tower for his final approach heading and landing instructions.

"Da Nang, Navy Claw 3, diverted from the USS Raleigh, landing with battle damage."

" Roger Claw 3, say your type."

"Da Nang, Navy A-4 Skyhawk," he called.

"Claw 3, are you declaring an emergency?"

Mathe had been schooled in whether or not to declare an emergency and understood the headaches that followed when one was announced—flying into this or any field for the Navy. Not only did he have a compromised jet, but his brakes were useless, and who knew what else, so he requested the midfield gear to be rigged. He would trap at Da Nang and hope for the best.

"Da Nang approach, that's Affirmative."

"Roger, Claw 3, continue Squawk 7700 and ident (signal your aircraft's identification code)."

Even with Marine skid (UH-1E, Huey) squadrons stationed at Marble Mountain, he was not sure he could stretch it. He had Finn's approximate location—so why not? He'd hump over to Marble after he landed. Sure, he'd flown the Huey, and if he had to he would borrow one to bring Finn back—but he thought his entry into Da Nang could be a little quieter.

Mathe was given emergency clearance for a straight-in on Runway 17R with the option for a midfield runway cable arrest.

Suddenly, "Claw 3, we are currently under attack and cannot recover your aircraft—suggest you contact Marble Mountain for your divert. We have notified them of your situation, Da Nang approach."

Suddenly, several golf ball-sized holes stitched across his wing and into the rear of his aircraft. Knowing that NVA forces often held the turf surrounding the airfield, he was not that surprised. Every nerve ending in his body was now alive.

Mathe gave two clicks of acknowledgment and confirmed his clearance with Marble Mountain approach.

"Hanging me out to dry, shit! Keep it together," Mathe mumbled.

Passing over Da Nang, he slowly decreased the power control lever to 60 percent, in preparation for his landing. The jet's RPMs (revolutions per minute), EGT(exhaust gas temperature of the turbine thrust) and EPR (pressure ratio as an indicator of thrust) readings fluctuated radically, and Mathe heard the first loud explosive pulse coming from the engine through the airframe—then nothing.

The jet had flamed out altogether. At a mile and half out from the Marble Mountain's runway he was now flying a brick at 900 hundred feet AGL. A total in-flight engine failure left him with few options at this altitude.

"Shit, no air start at this altitude, no airspeed to play with for a zoom climb," he mumbled.

Mathe instantly switched the fuel control to manual, and then hit the igniters while retarding the throttle to idle—then slowly advanced the throttle to determine thrust. Nothing.

He remembered his Air Force cross training—to take a moment to think about your options in an emergency, by "winding the clock," and then choose your course of action.

Without hesitation, he mumbled, "Time to leave."

After tightening his shoulder harness even tighter, he grabbed the face curtain handle, slid his heels back off the rudder pedals, and pulled hard and fast—*too fast*. Mathe was pissed that he couldn't seem to move soon enough to pull the ejection handle even though it was happening in a millisecond.

Nothing. No rocket fired. One hard pull on the curtain should do it—nothing!

Damn, this seat is going to kill me.

Mathe had one last option and reached for the alternate ejection handle and gave a strong, steady pull.

The seat rocket exploded—preceded by the canopy—up the rails and out. He and his seat flew over the tail of the airplane. What a kick in the butt and within two seconds, as advertised, he felt the reassuring pull of the risers and one swing to a hard landing.

The scooter went nose up and pivoted vertically for her final roll into the ground—straight into the red dirt of the Marble Mountain Marine base perimeter. The fireball from its impact sure was a sight.

Mathe momentarily lay in the warm, dusty earth while unclipping his Koch fittings from the billowing parachute. He quickly picked himself off the ground and started a fast walk directly to the flight line—trying to collect his thoughts. It looked like all hell was breaking loose with sirens, rescue trucks, and ambulance movement toward the rising column of smoke that marked his jet's grave—not far away. He broke into a run to hide from those trying to help him. A couple of hundred yards inside the perimeter, he hunkered down in a depression close to the runway as a Red Cross meat wagon passed beside on the nearby road. So far he had not been spotted and eventually found his old squadron's hangar and slowed to a fast walk to catch his breath.

His back was in pain but he kept himself straight— limping into the hangar area. He spotted Master Sergeant Benny Evangelista, his old-line mechanic, and approached him warily. Benny recognized Captain Stone instantly from his confident yet injured gate and dark features—outwardly, a bearing that projected real strength of character and confidence that under his CO's (Lieutenant Colonel McVey) command was sorely needed.

"Jesus, Skipper, how did you get here? You look terrible! I thought they transferred you to another squadron. "Well, they did, Benny—but right now can you get me into a fully serviced gunship? My best friend needs a rescue—right now!"

"Well, I don't know," Benny said, scratching his head again. "You know, Captain, you took me for everything I had at the poker table."

"I know, Benny, and I'll get it back to you."

"Hear those sirens? That smoke plume—is that for you? Everyone is going berzerk around here."

"Yep, looks like a rat fuck—just ejected off the perimeter," Mathe answered.

"You mean your plane is the one everyone is going crazy over. They must be looking for you, Captain." Benny scratched his head as was usual and took a hard look at his old friend.

"Look, Benny, I don't have time to talk about it. My best friend and squadron mate is down out there, and I need your help. He knows I'm coming. No one else will launch a RESCAP to save him now."

"Captain, do you have any idea the trouble that would come down on my head if I help you?"

"Yes, Benny, but I'm begging you," Mathe pleaded.

"I don't know. How long will you be gone?"

Mathe just shrugged and said, "Not long."

Benny held his breath. "Well—OK, I guess. See that one, Number 977?" He pointed to a fully fueled weather-beaten Huey down the flight line. "I think it's fixed, and I'll tell whoever asks that I thought it was being taken for a maintenance test flight, rescue or something."

As Mathe ran for the Huey, he yelled, "Thanks, Top, I owe you."

Time to break some rules, he thought.

The chaos of the stir Mathe had created on the airfield would be his cover, and their search on the ground would allow him to depart. After contacting ground control and then departure, he looked back at Benny, who was sheepishly peering from the hangar door as his career was passing before his eyes. Mathe reflected on how he missed the brotherhood, the Corps, and guys like Benny.

Benny was watching Captain Stone do his best imitation of a student pilot on his second training hop—better yet, his first hop at the controls. Even so, he liked the skipper and knew he was a hard charger. He had heard rumors that the captain had gotten a raw deal from Lieutenant Colonel McVey a while back, which caused his transfer, and he felt bad for him.

The controls of the Huey felt familiar and even somewhat enjoyable in the pressure of the moment, as Mathe pulled the eclectic and twisted in power for the lift-off. The chopper continued to skid-dance just above the ground, trying for an unusual attitude.

Mathe's radical initial control corrections became more deliberate as his helo piloting rust whirled away. Smoother control habits took hold as muscle memory kicked in. On his departure, things began to dampen out except for the incessant yelling from the tower—something about bringing the chopper back, about busted regulations, and more.

Mathe dialed in Finn's fix and tried to shut out the tower's noise. With continued questioning about his destination, which he chose to disregard, Mathe switched channels to contact Sea Biscuit.

Mathe explained his intent and indicated that the extent of Finn's injuries would most likely dictate his final destination after the rescue, as he tried to justify his actions. But, most importantly, he wanted to let them know that this was an unauthorized Marine Huey UH-1E RESCAP flight out of Marble Mountain and asked them to relay a message that *Claw 3 would not be reporting back* overhead the Raleigh—the next morning at seven. Departure indicated they would transmit the message, and Mathe knew all hell would break loose after this communication. It looked like it had already.

He knew this rescue was going to be tricky, to say the least. There was no contour map for the best point of landing or approach or course checkpoints for terrain clearance and authentication codes. None—just Finn's weakening calls and Mathe's eyeballs, which would be of little use in the fog. The Huey's inherent instability would be compounded by his inability to see outside the cockpit, but Finn was more than worth the risk. Mathe would be using Kamikaze tactics in this zero-visibility environment today. The Huey's limited IFR capabilities only added to the uncertainty of a fog-bank penetration.

Control of the machine and painful memories came back at about the same time as Mathe finally departed Marble airspace. It didn't take much for him to imagine the dead and bloody Marines stacked in the back of his ship—like the last mission he flew for the Corps, out of this airfield, a year and a half earlier.

Mathe passed over the smoke plume from his A-4 and the multitude of vehicles surrounding its demise and realized he was way ahead of the machine because of his pointy-end hangover. It was all coming back as he forced himself to slow down to match the somewhat relaxed demands of the machine he was driving and planning for what might happen during Finn's extraction.

It was the thought of McVey going ballistic when he heard Mathe's name and the fact that one of his skids just departed his airfield—unauthorized—that brought a smile to his face. Even though McVey was in a box, of Mathe's making, his teeth were sharp. Mathe knew he would pay a big price when he chewed his way into the truth of what happened to his base command—if they survived.

160

"So far, so good," he mumbled as he gained altitude and looked back at the door gunner's position.

It sure would have been good to have had some defensive support on this trip. As his back began to stiffen and spasm from the ejection, he motored on toward Finn's last fix. Off in the distance, the fog bank started to appear and hardened his resolve to rescue Finn. No low ceiling to duck under on this one—it went right to the ground.

Mathe couldn't save his mom or his dad, but this was his chance— to save his best friend. He motored to the fix in the thick, bright morning air, then made a 180 turn and committed to the descent.

* * *

Mathe was praying that he would regain visual contact with the ground in a good way as he eased the Huey slowly down into the fog bank. His stomach tightened with a familiar feeling as he fought the fear of what he couldn't see below.

"Claw 1, give me 20 seconds of beeper if able, Claw 3," Mathe called.

Finn heard the call, fumbled with his handheld survival radio, and acknowledged with his beeper.

"Copy your beeper, Claw 1," Mathe responded.

Suddenly Finn's attention was diverted to the *whomp, whomp, whomp* drumbeat sound of the Huey's rotor blades pounding the air in front of the machine.

Finn gathered all his strength as he limped out the door of the hut, with a slight nod to his captor. His eyes bugged in physical shock and fear while he tried to suppress his pain. His head swiveled as he looked for anyone who threatened to intercept his course to the plateau.

Finn had made two calls before Mathe had departed the area in his A-4, just south of his position. The beeper fix on Finn's location was reliable. Finn radioed again on Mathe's approach for the pickup, saying he should be able to walk out of the village and that there were no NVA (regular North Vietnam Army troops) in the area yet—just farmers holding him for something or someone.

Mathe neared Finn's position. His radio was set to Finn's emergency frequency. Mathe keyed three clicks to signal his arrival. Finn responded with three and Mathe asked him about his location. He whispered that he had Mathe in sight and was hunkered down by the riverbank one hundred yards south of him and was on his way.

"How bad are you hurt? Any NVA close? I'm looking," Mathe hurriedly responded as he heard the distinctive crack of an AK-47 opening up.

Mathe squinted through the mist and finally sighted the ground. As he touched down hard, right side up, he spotted Finn across the plateau, desperately limping for his life—more than ready to leave. AK-47 rounds began to impact the ground around him as he ran for his escape from the village hut hidden beside the tree line. Mathe jumped for the M-60 door gun and, with no real targets, cocked the gun to the direction of the tree line and opened up with alternating bursts between the streambed and the tree line beside the hill. It was hard to pinpoint the exact location of the gomers doing the firing—the jungle looked the same wherever you looked. Turning away made it even harder to pinpoint the enemy, even after seeing a flash.

He kept firing—not allowing them to target Finn running for his life.

"Keep coming, Finn! Got you in sight—move man, move! "

Finn suddenly went forward, stumbling to the ground either from being hit or sheer exhaustion. Mathe sent out another burst, then leaped from the side door and humped the 30 yards to his side.

As Mathe hit the dirt beside Finn, he gave him a weak smile. Finn looked beat up and smelled like hell with a dirt-encrusted gash across his cheek. He was blood-soaked and rice paddy excrement smelly—but alive!

"You seem to be in a bit of trouble Lieutenant. You want to get outta here?" Mathe encouraged. "Let's go, partner. Time to leave."

He looked like he was about to pass out any second.

"Come on, we can do this," Mathe said as he lifted Finn one arm at a time.

"Saved by the Corps—you're kidding me. You da man—you first, Rock," Finn disjointedly stammered through his exhaustion and pain.

Finn gave Mathe a pained grin and somehow as they ran/crawled across the plain—as rounds continued impacting the ground at their heels and into the UH1-E Huey helicopter with rotors spinning. While running, Mathe turned and fired scattered shots at the tree line with his trusty .357 Magnum personal sidearm, still hoping to buy time by keeping their heads down. Throwing Finn into the back, Mathe jumped for the cockpit and full-on lifted out from the hornet's nest as holes began to appear everywhere—a frightening but familiar sight.

The Huey, laden with moisture and Math's bloodied squadron mate as cargo, finally popped out of the dense fog bank and into bright sunshine. Mathe turned around again and noticed Finn's blood loss on the floor of the Huey.

Automatically, Mathe changed channels to Raleigh's approach frequency. In the back of his mind, he started wondering if Finn had punctured a major artery. No time to check—had to get out of there.

Damn. These thoughts scared the shit out of him—losing his best friend—no fucking way!

Even so, Mathe decompressed a tad—more than halfway home.

"Hang in there, Finn!"

The scent of sea salt and cooler air assaulted their senses, as they went feet wet over the ocean blue on a direct course for the Raleigh. Mathe looked back at his buddy once more—hoping.

"How are you doing, Finn?" he asked. There was no answer.

Twenty-One: One Ton's Pay Back

The Coin Flip
"Respect" – Aretha Franklin

HMM- 332 Headquarters – Da Nang

"He took what? Just flew one of our UH-1s off the field after he cracked up the A-4?" Lieutenant Colonel McVey was rapidly reddening as he spoke to his master sergeant.

Benny Evangelista stood at attention in front of McVey. "Colonel, I," and his words tailed off. He bent his head forward, looking at the Quonset floor, and paused mid-sentence.

"Goddamnit, Sergeant, how did you let him get away with this? Have you lost what small mind you have left?" McVey screamed as his face finally turned to beet red with anger.

"Colonel, is this the captain that transferred out of the squadron a few years ago?" Benny stammered, knowing full well that McVey had called for his demise. He was trying to change McVey's line of questioning.

Two inches from Benny's face, McVey pounced. "He seems to be headed north into zero-zero visibility to the northwest, a fog bank. What's he up to? Doesn't the Navy have another A-4 down in that area?" McVey continued to hammer Benny. He was looking for a way and a decision that would limit his exposure to failure—out of the box Captain Stone had placed him in with his actions today.

"Two aircraft down in two hours—what a cluster fuck!"

"I guess so, sir, but he can't fly into that stuff—it's impossible. He'll kill himself. Maybe we should send someone after him."

"No, Master Sergeant, absolutely not! These aircraft cost money you know! I'm calling Raleigh's air boss. This pilot is dangerous enough. Any calls from FACs in the northern area yet?"

Raleigh (CVA-23)

Upon being notified of the loss of two aircraft and the unusual circumstance surrounding an apparent SAR (search and rescue) on board the Raleigh, Admiral McCready, commanding officer of the carrier strike group, immediately requested a pick up from his flagship to meet the flyers personally on the Raleigh.

After coming on board the Raleigh, Admiral "One Ton" McCready found his way to Captain Leader's quarters. He sat down at Leader's desk, fuming. *Stone again? Jesus. Give me a break!* A knock at Leader's door broke his thoughts.

"Admiral, we have an incoming Marine helicopter flown by Captain Stone with Lieutenant Finley aboard. Stone is requesting landing approval and medical personnel at the ready," the sailor announced above the din of onboard operations.

"He's flying what?" McCready asked, suddenly remembering Stone's background as a CH-46 driver and his previous dust-up with McVey.

"Tell him to land that thing and get his ass in here!" McCready yelled.

"Tell DCAG (deputy air wing commander) Kilkenny, to clear the deck. Have Stone report to me, in my cabin, as soon as they touch down and tell him Admiral McCready would like a chat with him.

"Have Captain Leader square Lieutenant Finley away with medical. I'll talk to Finley later if he is able."

Admiral McCready got up from the desk in Leader's quarters and found his way to the bridge and leaned over to Captain Leader and Deputy Commander Kilkenny, and whispered, "Gentlemen, meet me in Leader's quarters when they land."

Pilots labeled him "One Ton" because he was known to bring a ton of hurt down on those who had screwed up. The admiral, with his thick New England accent, had steam coming out of his ears. DCAG Kilkenny on the other hand, had grown up in Ohio and held his Midwestern cards close to his chest. Even though it was consensus by the junior officers that he was "solid stick," his decisions were a bit quirky at times. Even so, their belief in him as a leader was solid.

"McCready stomped off the bridge mumbling, "Goddamnit—insubordination, hijacking government property, wrecking government property—two A-4's down and then a stolen helicopter! Disobeying orders—not this shit again."

* * *

"Hawk Approach, Claw 3 is up," Mathe called.

"Roger, Claw 3, we have you painted."

With desperate urgency, Mathe called again, "Hawk approach, request a ready deck. Wounded aboard."

"Roger, Claw 3, your signal Charley, come aboard."

Mathe landed and made sure medical help arrived for Finn's injuries. He knew what was coming but was more concerned about

167

Finn. Unconscious now, they took him away on a stretcher—a bloody mess.

Still high on adrenaline, Mathe was directed to the admiral's quarters. He could not believe that an admiral was on board and wanted to speak with him. His first wrap on the admiral's door brought a firm "Enter."

Admiral McCready looked up from Leader's desk with steely eyes. Beside him sat Captain Leader and DCAG Kilkenny. There was no humor in their demeanors today—they were boiling. Mathe caught Commander Kilkenny's stern grimace.

He stood at attention and saluted. "Sir, Captain Stone reporting as ordered."

"You have some explaining to do, Captain."

Admiral "One Ton" McCready never pulled punches. Everything Mathe knew about the admiral was positive. He was a, *It's what you do—not the way that you do it type*—a real doer.

Officers and sailors alike said, 'When he shakes your hand and he says something to you, you look at him and immediately recognize that he's the real deal. He's about as genuine as they come—nothing fake and no one wants to let him down.'

Even though they had never met, Mathe respected him because of his reputation and rank. He had *tried* to live by the same code himself.

This perceived understanding of the admiral's character was a slim handle to hold onto as he stood at attention and waited for the worst. It stiffened his painful spine and created a willingness to accept his fate. "One Ton" would demand respect, professionalism, and humility, and Mathe had no other choice. *Whatever was headed his way today*, he thought, could not compare to the last 12 hours.

His decision to save Finn was the right choice even though he knew he was dancing on thin ice.

"It seems you have had a busy day, Captain. Do you want to tell us about it? No, let me. You take off in an A-4 and return flying a Huey. Hung ordinance, my ass!" he barked.

Mathe launched into the explanation. "Yes, well, sir—about that," he stuttered.

"One Ton" promptly cut him off in midsentence. He already knew the truth.

"Captain, I have an enraged lieutenant colonel in Da Nang who needs some answers—more like a large piece of your ass. You do know who I am referring to, don't you?"

"Ah, yes, sir. I do."

"Take a seat, Captain. This may take some time because you are going to give me every last detail of this charade you pulled off— Not just two missing A-4s but a Marine helicopter. NOW!"

Definitely in the hot seat now—time to come clean, he thought to himself.

What Mathe did not know was that the admiral had flown with Mathe's dad in WWII and Korea. Mathe's dad was the reason McCready was still alive. McCready knew that Mathe had crossed swords with McVey in the past and had saved Mathe's career then, with his transfer to the Talons. He never discussed it with Mathe. There was so much Captain Stone didn't know. This was a second opportunity to support him—but not before he took a piece of him.

Mathe gulped, took a deep breath, and said, "Admiral, Lieutenant Finley is in rough shape. The rescue was the right thing to do, and he needs immediate medical attention. Can…" The admiral cut him off again.

169

Like preparing for some strange bedtime story, the atmosphere in the room suddenly changed.

"Captain, we're taking good care of Lieutenant Finley."

"One Ton" suddenly reached for a box on the desk, pulled out three cigars, lit one up, and passed the others to Captain Leader and DCAG Kilkenny. Mathe slowly lost some of that prickly fear he'd brought in the door with him.

Is he really breaking the distance? Mathe wondered.

"Now, go ahead, Captain. We're all ears," the admiral said as a cloud of cigar smoke broiled over Mathe.

"Well, sir, Finn's jet was shot up pretty bad. He took rounds through the canopy, and the aft end of his jet was shot up. He had a partially deployed slat with fuel streaming out of the back of the scooter. I didn't think he could make it back, let alone get clearance to come aboard. Lieutenant Finley disappeared in the fog bank and my jet was in rough shape too from a missile strike and I requested a divert to Da Nang."

McCready could see Mathe's disjointed nervous response and sought to settle him down.

"Stop, Captain. Take us back again to your beginning with Lieutenant Finley."

"How far back, sir?" Mathe broke eye contact, with his head down. "We have a lot of history."

Mathe told of their friendship before and during their military careers—even though he was not really sure if they wanted to hear all their adventures. He continued with the bones of today's debacle, and the admiral interrupted.

"If I read you right, do you think your jet flamed out because of the fuel metering problems we've had or because of enemy fire within the immediate Da Nang area? Captain, your divert to Da Nang didn't have anything to do with Lieutenant Finley's situation, did it?"

Caught! Time for the whole truth, Mathe thought.

"Well, yes. It did, sir. I could tell from the way his jet was behaving that Finn had more problems than just what the jet was dictating. He was wounded, as his cockpit was holed out. He was having problems communicating—he needed immediate help, sir! When he disappeared into the fog bank and I caught what I thought was the flash of his ejection, I realized I had to rescue him at any cost. Da Nang was the closest emergency field. After being vectored to Marble Mountain, my jet quit. I barely got there—she flamed—and I had to eject just short of the field. My old squadron was still stationed there. The stir that was created by my jet going down and my ejection allowed me time to 'borrow' a UH-1 and depart the field for Finn's location— well, more like hijack the Huey, I guess."

"An individual SAR? You alone, no support?" the admiral drilled.

"Well, yes, sir, yes," Mathe stuttered again.

"So you stole the Huey and departed unauthorized on a rescue mission, into zero-zero conditions with no support and little or no communication?"

"Sir, I thought I could get him. I knew where he was and I took the chance even though the coin had not flipped in my favor," he sputtered.

Suddenly, the admiral stood, looked over at DCAG Kilkenny and Captain Leader and said, "Gentlemen, may I have a moment alone with the captain?"

The Raleigh's captain and deputy commander immediately grabbed their coffee mugs and vacated their seats, closing the door quietly behind them. Mathe's stomach tightened even more.

Admiral McCready told him to sit.

171

"Join me, son," he said, as he pulled out a fourth cigar and passed it across his desk.

This was getting even more bizarre, he thought.

"Ah—thank you, Admiral," Mathe hesitantly responded, not sure what was going on.

Mathe looked into the admiral's eyes and braced for the worst. He had never spoken to an admiral—let alone Admiral McCready. This was his first chance to speak with him in person, and the circumstances left much to be desired. He waited for the admiral to play his hand for a better read of where he stood. Both kibbitzed back and forth and talked about the squadron, Mathe's CO, and his friendship with Finn.

Mathe was slowing coming off the edge of the biggest day of his life—no matter how it would end—as the adrenaline slowly oozed away. Fatigue was settling in.

The cigar certainly helped him muster the courage to speak openly. What did he have to lose? More importantly, he had the feeling that his actions today were partially accepted. The admiral's tone still held a threatening edge and had him guessing. He had the flag power to crush his career, instantly.

"Last question, Captain. Did you hit the target?"

"Oh, yes, sir," he said with a smile. "I'll provide a complete report for you."

"That was a pretty rich tale you just told, Captain. Some gutsy choices. Heroic of you to rescue your flight lead Lieutenant Finley. Does the fact that you grew up together play a significant factor in putting your career on the line?"

"Well, yes, sir, that was part of it, but he was wounded and my squadron mate. There was no chance for an immediate RESCAP in that weather—I couldn't just leave him."

A slow smile began to appear on the admiral's face.

"One Ton" knew he had taken enough chunks out of Stone today, and now he would throw the weight of his rank behind this young flyer, again.

"Good job, Captain, risking your life to save Lieutenant Finley. We are all proud of you, regardless of your methods."

McCready suddenly remembered his past discussions with McVey and smiled, at the thought of tangling with him again.

"Captain, your squadron commander is about to start a ceremony for Claw flight. You need to be there. You need to get to the Talons ready room. However, before you go, I have a story for you about your dad. But that can wait."

Mathe was aghast. He had no words.

"My dad?" *What does he know about my Dad? I don't understand.* And then the Admiral dismissed him just like that.

* * *

A cloud of cigar smoke enveloped the sweat-soaked aviators as they celebrated their victory. Not one pilot had lost or smoked his cheroot, except one, prior to the celebration except for Mathe, who was too busy accepting congratulations to light up the cigar that he'd already smoked. The Talons' first kill by Lieutenant Chavez and Mathe's heroic save of Finn spread like wildfire over the ship, and all sailors walked with a touch more swagger than usual for a few days—before the daily grind caught back up with them. Even so, Finn's health was in question as they transferred him ashore for medical attention—he had come back to the ship in rough shape. The Talons partied like rock stars again in their next port—U.S. Naval Air Station Cubi

Point—and Olongapo City was never quite the same after their celebration.

Rumor had it that over 1,500 Air Force "Thud" pilots had lost either their lives or were imprisoned in Hanoi along with their Navy brethren. The war had become ugly and controversial as friends were lost but the Talons' kept doing their jobs—each pilot inflicting pain and death from the air.

By early 1975 the conflict was finally coming to a close and many of Finn's and Mathe's squadron mates would be cycling to other assignments in the Navy. Others simply left active service for civilian careers—in the so called real world.

Twenty-Two: True Blues

Finn lost one testicle and had a nice battle scare on his face—something for which he showed a lot of quiet pride.

After recuperating at Walter Reed for several months, he was assigned orders to the Naval Postgraduate School at Monterey and later received a degree from the Army War College. He was screened for command and became executive officer of an East Coast A-6 squadron, which was eventually deployed to sea.

Mathe was selected and received orders to join the Blue Angels Flight Demonstration Team. Captain Matthew Stone transitioned out of VA-104 Talons and became a newbie again on this elite team—even though he was a seasoned aviator and fit the Angel mold. Mathe integrated well with the team—as the lone Marine.

Several months into his assignment with the "Blues" Mathe gave Finn a call to catch up and pass on a story. The team's slot pilot—Don "Mud Skunk" O'Shea had also suffered the loss of a testicle from his Vietnam War years. Mathe was excited to tell him that if Finn joined the team he could help them fly their signature four-plane diamond (eight balls) formation except with six balls. He knew that Mud

Skunk's testicle loss had not affected his concentration nor inhibited his performance in other realms. Since both O'Shea and Finn had become fathers—it was proof that one works just as well as two.

After two seasons with the "Blues," 5.2 years of active service, two cruises, and two full workup cycles with over 1100 hours flight time, and 345 carrier landings Mathe chose to enter civilian life.

He left "The NAV" for a job in the Chevrolet Marketing Information Systems Center working for a guy named DeLorean. The transition was not easy. Even though he lamented that GM was trying to turn him into a clerk, he continued to fly everything he could get his hands on in his off time—as a pilot in the Naval Reserves.

Mathe went on to marry Rusty, and they raised Carolyn and Matthew Jr. He did not care whether they ever flew for the Navy or at all. He did encourage both of his kids to pick up a lacrosse stick and enjoy the "spirit of the stick."

Mathe held onto his naval reserve officer designation tightly—a title given to him by Congress that he took very seriously. That title allowed him to push the envelope—like he always had. After all, he was a Naval Aviator.

Epilogue

"Adagio for Strings" – London Philharmonic Orchestra

They had traveled here many times before. The view of the Italian peaks was just as amazing this time and being here still had the same effect—energizing and so beautiful. Mathe shivered a bit from the high-altitude cold as the discomfort from the rock he was sitting on continued to penetrate his butt.

"Living as we did, you wouldn't think we could have gotten this far—what a view—still incredible!"

"You still with me, pal."

"Yep, I'm here."

Mathe sat with his thoughts until the voice piped in again.

"At least I don't have to worry about outliving my Johnson. Rusty, have any complaints?"

Mathe laughed to himself and smiled.

"Not so far, but thanks for your concern, One Nut."

They knew each other too well—were a part of each other. Two sides to the same coin.

"Mathe, pull that cap a little lower over your severely bald head. Without hair up there you will give brain freeze a new definition."

"Hey, hot dog, let's not get carried away," Mathe resounded.

And so it went on until Mathe had to pry his body off the rock and start the long climb down.

The summit perch was magnificent, but daylight was more precious now. The lower part of the mountain was covered in green with tall pines—in stark contrast to the line of snow-capped peaks that traveled to the south east from his position.

Mathe stared at the mountains, whose peaks seemed to pierce the sky—just to burn the view into his mind.

He remembered Finn by his side, not so long ago, during his own chemo sessions, and wished he could have helped Finn survive his battle with cancer.

"Damn Disease!"

The mountains gave Mathe one more chance to meet and touch their high-altitude worlds.

As he sought his path downward he turned to look one more time. He knew it wasn't possible, but....

There, just for a moment, he saw him, young, smiling and full of life. Finn popped a salute, flipped him the bird and—was gone.

A smile spread across Mathe's face.

I miss you, Finn!

* * *

At 53, Finn and his family retired from the military. Mathe helped them move into a house only two blocks away from his family's home. Maddy and Rusty became the best of friends. All eight of them had many amazing times together—hiking, biking, camping and much more.

Finn passed way too early and was buried at Arlington, not because he was a big-time hero but because he deserved it. Both families' said goodbye to him on a beautiful day in May and left him there in very good company.

He had done some amazing things in his long military career. But, that never went to his head—always just a regular guy who happened to be able to fly the shit out of anything.

Maddy is still on her own but the kids keep her busy. She says she is a "one-man woman" and that is that.

For Mathe, seeing his best friend go was the worst. He could never figure out why Finn went before him. "Why him and not me," was heard often by his family, in his quiet moments.

A-4 Skyhawk

The A-4 light attack aircraft was built as a nuclear-attack capable light bomber. It was the U.S. Navy's most utilized bomber during the Vietnam War. It was small, agile, maneuverable, and rugged.

Supported by fighters, the Skyhawk flew its bombing missions deep into Southeast Asian airspace in ground attack missions over both North and South Vietnam.

It was affectionately called the "The Scooter," designed by Ed Heinemann and built by Douglas Aircraft. It served the U.S. Navy and Marine Corps from 1956 onward for nearly 40 years.

About The Author

D. Stuart White is an author, business development consultant, entrepreneur, consumer behavior analyst, commercial pilot, lacrosse coach, and lifelong aviation and military history buff. White contributes to a variety of publications.

He is best known for his in-depth organizational development case studies and articles that include the lessons learned from military aviation personnel transitions to corporate environments. His flight experience includes PIC flight time in multiple corporate, civil, and military aircraft.

He is a Michigan State University graduate, served as a naval officer, and lives in Bloomfield Hills, Michigan, with his wife, Ann.

wa2dsw@gmail.com
https://www.linkedin.com/in/
https://twitter.com/DStuartWhite2
https://www.dstuartwhite.com/

Thank You!

If you enjoyed the book I would be thankful if you would consider posting a review on Amazon.com.

Your positive review will help Amazon get the book in front of more people who also might enjoy the novel.

And *Thank You* again for reading *Tall Air!*